# The Death of an Author

S. L. Edwards

**JOURNALSTONE**
YOUR LINK TO ARTIST TALENT

ISBN: 978-1-950305-88-9 (sc)
ISBN: 978-1-950305-89-6 (ebook)
Library of Congress Control Number: 2021940697
First printing edition: June 25, 2021
Published by JournalStone Publishing in the United States of America.
Cover Design / Author Photo: Yves Tourigny | Layout: Scarlett R. Algee
Edited by Sean Leonard
Proofreading and Interior Layout by Scarlett R. Algee

JournalStone Publishing
3205 Sassafras Trail
Carbondale, Illinois 62901

JournalStone books may be ordered through booksellers or by contacting:
JournalStone | www.journalstone.com

To Dad, for all his time.

Introduction by John Linwood Grant

## Part I: Fantasies and True Secrets

I.     Christmas at Castle Dracula (originally published in *Weirdbook Magazine #41*, Wildside Press) **15**

II.     Allister's Garden (originally published in *Unleashed: Monsters vs. Zombies, Vol. II*) **21**

III.     A Slower Way of Starving (original to this collection) **33**

IV.     She Never Killed Spiders (originally published in *Mythic Magazine #6*, Founders House Publishing LLC) **48**

V.     Bestia (original to this collection) **61**

VI.     With All Her Troubles Behind Her (originally published in *Test Patterns: Creature Features*, Planet X Publications) **76**

VII.     I Keep It in a Little Box (originally published in *32 White Horses on a Vermillion Hill Vol. 1*, Planet X Publications) **90**

VIII.     The Death of an Author (originally published in *Mythic Magazine #4*, Founders House Publishing LLC) **103**

IX.     Standing There (original to this collection) **113**

X.     Christmas Alone (original to this collection) **115**

## Part II: Miskatonic and Madness

XI.     The Cthulhu Candidate (originally published in *Ravenwood Quarterly #2*, Ravenwood Books) **121**

XII.     Office Hours and After (originally published in *It Came from Miskatonic!*, Broken Eye Books) **130**

XIII.     The Referendum Over Innsmouth (original to this collection) **146**

XIV.     The Ambassador in Yellow (original to this collection) **156**

XV.     The Darkness Makes Us Whole (originally published in *Miskatonic Dreams*, Alban Lake Books) **164**

## Part III: Brief Goodbyes

XVI.     Afterword **191**

XVII.     The Last Mayflies out of Bogota (original to this collection) **193**

XVIII.     About the Author

# Introduction

EVERYTHING YOU THINK you know about S. L Edwards is wrong. Assuming, that is, you think him to be a part-time pool-cleaner from Alberta who writes Hallmark movies in his spare moments. If, on the other hand, you think that he's a rising author of dark fictions, then you've beaten the odds and found yourself someone well worth investigating.

I say rising because he only came fully to the table over the last few years, but has already drawn attention. It is usually a pleasure to welcome such emerging writers into the world of horror and weird fiction, if only to pass on inaccurate information and failed techniques, in the hope that you can stop them before they get better at it than you.

Sadly, every so often there comes along one such writer who ignores your attempts at sabotage, and survives, even thrives, in the blood-drenched world of authorial malice.

S. L Edwards is one of those annoyingly tenacious souls.

Taking as his spirit animal the noble and ingenious armadillo of his beloved Texas, he has armoured himself against outrageous misfortune; he has prospered to such an extent that I, in providing this introduction, am relegated to warming up a bemused audience before the main turn, like the ageing vaudeville act I resemble. Not only that, but this is no first foray; it is in fact Sam's second collection of strange and worrying tales.

I should not have been entirely surprised at such a turn of events. His remark "John, I'm releasing a second collection," gave me my first, subtle clue. There were other hints, of course—in my role as itinerant editor, I had the pleasure of publishing a number of his stories, notably in the anthology 'Hell's Empire' and in various issues of *Occult Detective Magazine*. I had also dipped into his contributions to a range of other venues, and I knew, therefore, that he was building up a considerable body of work.

So, I was familiar with his fiction in general—a blend of contemporary weird and thoughtful horror, sometimes bloody but never Grand Guignol. On those occasions where a hack or a slash is required, there are deep-seated reasons, reasons more important than the act itself—Sam deals with motivations more than morgues.

What would this new venture bring? The stories which follow are undoubtedly 'Edwards' stories, yet they provide fresh twists and turns as well. Such twists and turns are particularly striking in the first part of this book, where he toys with the world of mythologies, and utilises a process of deconstruction and reconstruction to yield surprising results. Here we are treated to a collection within a collection, *Fantasies and True Secrets*, where draculas and pandoras emerge as familiar strangers; beauties consort with beasts (no, not like that), whilst zombies and dragons share a world of pain. Tropes are wrenched; the nature of authority—just who is in charge?—is challenged, and captivity and suffering reign.

In fact, suffering is the order of the day. Whilst the question of what comes next is often left open, the parts of the journey we see are pretty rough. Many people struggle and die in Edwards stories; even if the protagonist manages to make it, they're rarely 'free' by any normal definition of the word. There are few innocents, and even mythically speaking, there are few heroes in the sense you know them. Those who survive are either changed, or they are more deeply confirmed on a path which may seem—to them—inevitable.

"They made you what you are so that you could *suffer*. Because you *deserve* it!" ('With All Her Troubles Behind Her')

Only in one tale, the eponymous 'Death of an Author," does he open the shutters fully to let light into the room, and this is a short break only, for the second substantial section, *Miskatonic and Madness*, deals with a more recent form of mythology, taking Lovecraftian or Mythosian concepts and extrapolating them into the modern world.

Edwards has long had an abiding interest in the impact of political systems, both on those who wield power and those who struggle under it (based, I have heard, on his years teaching Anarcho-Syndicalist Theory to the Galveston Junior Chipmunks). Here he eschews the fields of Central and Southern American politics, which have featured in a number of powerful stories of his to be found elsewhere, and turns instead to a meld of Mythosian corruption and the nature of contemporary machinations in the United States.

This meld is complemented by forays into good old Miskatonic University (as you might have guessed) for some distinctly dark outings, taking further Lovecraftian elements and baring the knife. *Miskatonic and Madness* contains many teasing, and some tart, references to HPL's original material, but never seeks to be pastiche. It's a fresh take, dragged very much into the 21st century, and the better for it.

And what has all the above to do with price of fish? Well, I hope that this collection will intrigue, satisfy, even provide the occasional wry smile at its convolutions, but most of all, it will sometimes discomfort – which is what this stuff is supposed to do. So put your hands together, please, for that recently-arrived star in a fearsome firmament, Mr. Edwards, a fine writer surely with much more yet to come...

*John Linwood Grant*
*Yorkshire*
*February 2021*

# The
# Death
## of an
# Author

# Part I: Fantasies and True Secrets

# Christmas at Castle Dracula

YOU BELIEVE THAT I am evil.

I can tell by your eyes. So pointed, so full of hatred, bile, and revulsion. You look at me and you see innumerable sins, unforgivable crimes against both your species and your God.

This is fine. I do not blame you. You will have time to come to understand me, my friend. And I *do* consider you my friend, despite what you might think. We have already been through so much in your days here, and you are not going anywhere any time soon.

You will thank me after, when all of this is over.

But before that, I want to tell you that you misunderstand me. You hold up your cross and you believe that I cower away in fear, in vulnerability. But I will tell you, it is not with fear that I look upon the sword of God...it is with *reverence*. I look upon this instrument of torture, this symbol of the cruelty mankind inflicts on anything it sees as greater and more divine than itself, and I feel *kindred*.

I was just a child when my *devout* Christian father gave my brother and I to *devout* Muslims in slavery. It is no wonder that when I finally returned home I acted so cruelly. In their dungeons I learned hatred, the sort of hatred an animal adopts in its cage. It does not know why, it does not know how, but the caged animal knows that *something is not right*. It knows it does *not* belong in a cage. So it paces back and forth, biting at every hand, whether they feed it or beat it.

To be certain, our cages were gilded, our jailers thought themselves merciful men. Eventually we were removed from the dungeons and placed amongst a sort of limited society. They taught us things which they should have not. Arts of horsemanship, literature, their very language.

But above all else, their cruelty.

The cruelty by which, despite any other virtue, I will always remember them.

They would open our doors at night and whisper into our ears, as we cried, that it was our *privilege* to be their prisoners.

They taught me more there, more than my brother, who came to love his captors more than he ever loved our family. I do not blame him, given the loyalty of our father. But I never could understand, and I never could sympathize with his choice. I loved my brother and deeply wish that I had been a better keeper.

If there is one regret which immortality has given me, it is that I bear upon myself the mark of Cain.

I prayed often there. To my God, to my father. Little did I know, my father was no godly man. And my God was always with me.

Our captors released me onto the world and I brought with me the hatred which had grown for so long. You look at me now and I know you see a monster. But you are born of the sins of monsters such as myself. What is the difference between the impalement of a hundred men, the slaughter of widows and children, compared to the suffering of one child? You look upon me and see some Eastern barbarian, some vaguely Asiatic warlord. You put distance between yourself and me, but you do not take into account the sins of your own fathers. Surely you must look upon what your country has done in India, and certainly you must know what happened to the people who stood to protect their homes when your ships arrived. And in these actions, my dear friend, you may believe that you see my influence on history. But this is not the case.

I was a man before I was ever any sort of "monster."

How shocking is a banquet amongst corpses when every meal, every success and excess you consume is built upon the lives and sufferings of millions?

I have given you much to think about. I pray you consider it while you hang there. I encourage you to sleep. It will make the time go so much faster.

I will return when I can. Goodnight.

···

Greetings, my friend. You look much better. The change will progress, will heal you.

I, however, must apologize.

I never wished to make another man my prisoner.

You might perceive hypocrisy, and you would not be entirely wrong. I was still a man when I was *voivode*. Murder, slaughter, genocide. These were small concerns in one of the bloodiest tracts of land in my time. The dirt at the crossroads of civilizations is always hungry and must be watered accordingly. I was made to believe that I was part of a great clash of two civilizations, and that I was the tortured child of both.

And despite all of the garments and vestments, I had given up on God. I was a faithless man in the armor of the faith, a wolf in sheep's clothing. My animal hatred burned against every Turk who represented my childhood jailers, against every European who represented the godless father who so willingly surrendered my innocence.

But then, this changed on the road from Bucharest to Giurgiu.

There, I beheld the same blinding light that Saul had beheld before he became Paul. I was thrown from my horse, crushed underneath and killed in the light of something far greater than any man could ever be.

Surely, my friend, you have read the word. But to read of the resurrection is one thing; to experience it is another entirely. I have looked upon the word with eyes which have truly been reborn and I have seen the secret meanings passed down to those given the true gift of eternity on earth. There are scripts there, invisible to those who are confined to a mortal life. Between the lines, in the sacred and hidden meter of the truly divine.

Now...looking back on my past as Saul, I see that mankind will always attempt to consume itself. Every man alive is a Cain, and any Abel is slaughtered long before he has time to become old.

The differences you make between yourselves are truly superficial, purely cosmetic. The blood of an Englishman tastes the same as any other. Inside each of you are a series of innards, defined not by any nationhood but by *pipework*.

And yet you cannot overcome your differences because you are born into them, inheriting the prejudices of generations before. And so, burdened with ancestral hatreds, you and your leaders will always seek to begin wars over small infractions, matters of ego, and fabricated prides.

When I awoke, after decades of cold, long darkness, I climbed my way from my tomb and held myself up in the mountains, in the ruins of my old life. And there I studied, grew, and waited with my new form. The word was a frequent subject of study, and I grew more sympathetic to a God willing to suffer for his world rather than condemn it. And I studied languages, philosophy; for a hundred years I lived alone with my library.

It is true, though, that eternity requires a sacrifice, requires a devotion and commitment which would make the lesser folk tremble. I sought to pass eternity on to those worthy. Those who were not worthy...they were only men, only women. I climbed down from my tower walls, slithered into their villages, and killed them as they slept. And as I did so, I whispered prayers and thanks into their ears, sending them on their way to their maker with mercy and blessings.

You call vampirism a sickness and you are as blinded by prejudice as your species ever was. It is pure, unabashed egotism to think yourselves the superior creatures on this planet. How can an entire species, an entire race, be a *disease?* We will burn in the sunlight, surely, but we will not die by gunshot, nor by any of the other ailments which make humanity so frail. We need the blood of others, but no water, no food. You think of our existence as impossible, as a wretched contamination. However, we are in fact the *advancement* of the human race.

We are far more *holy.*

Think on my words. I will see you tomorrow night.

...

You might think it strange, my friend, but I do not hold any ill will towards those who have killed me.

Each time, I learn something new: a vulnerability which I was unaware of or a method that somehow escaped mention in any of my books. Then, when this information is passed down to the inevitable children of those who will oppose me, I will be more prepared. In this way, I owe you and the others many thanks.

And then, each time I die, I come closer to my Lord.

Death is only a temporary pain, after all. It is one which, as you see, can be recovered from.

But those who fight me look upon me and they see what you see. They compare me to Genghis, to Napoleon. But I tell you now, that in all the history of this world you will have never seen a ruler such as a Dracula. Never before has one been so clearly sent by their maker to dominate and lead mankind.

I will take control of this world; the matter merely lies in the waiting.

And that is precisely the problem with humans, with leaders of men. They are made of breakable bones, malleable minds, and conquerable spirits. They only live so long before they make their irreparable mistakes, and not knowing the extent of history which years of studies brings, they commit the same errors as their fathers. They spend the blood of sons, the lives of men and women, on things which they do not need. Their sight only extends years, decades if a man is truly wise. But a decade is no time at all to someone who does not die, or to someone who will not *stay* dead. And the preservation of your children will be a very different cause than the preservation of your great-great grandchildren, ancestors who you will never know.

But I will know them.

We will not make humanity cattle. The notion is ridiculous. Our culture would thrive by night but be dead during the day, our planet would be losing half of its time. It is true, though, that we will need to feed. And we will not apologize for this. There are more than enough people on this planet to feed every vampire for over a century. And at the rate populations grow, the more we seem a natural check. They will die, and it will be necessary. Progress has always come at the price of blood, and the end of history is no different than what preceded it.

But we will not turn them into us. Should we do that, there would be too many of us.

And then we would become them, we would become mankind. With all of its fictitious schisms and all of its careless violence.

No...no, I am content to rule from a distance, content to sit on an invisible throne with my shadow-laden crown. I need nothing more from my subjects than that blood which I must take to survive. I am willing to outweigh the lifespan of nations, of empires, of any of those who have any hope of killing me. And when they are gone, I will give their children...my children, a new earth.

Here, drink. This is the blood of my covenant, which is poured out for you.

Eat. My flesh, given for you.
Sleep well, friend, for when you wake it will be with new eyes.
Welcome to my home. To *your* home.
And, of course, merry Christmas.

**Author's Notes:** Everyone knows Dracula. From Western pop-literature, he always seemed as iconic (if not more) than Sherlock Holmes. His long teeth, red eyes, theatrical cape. He's been interpreted, adapted, over and over again.

I wanted my Dracula to be a terrifying character, not because he was drinking blood and crawling along tower walls, but because he was a conqueror. And not just a conqueror, but someone who promised paradise out of a long, brutal pain.

I'm not sure where the idea of setting this story in Christmas came from, but the real story of Vlad Tepes falling off of his horse seemed to me too much like the story of Saul becoming Paul. I couldn't pass it up.

# Allister's Garden

THE GARDEN RADIATES with decay and roses. The anarchic artificial jungle, where wild and domesticated plants desperately choke each other for light and dirt, is contained in an imposing black iron cage. It is a massive thing, at least twelve feet tall and twenty feet wide, with gaps so small that only the thinnest vines and fingers poke through in a desperate climb for sunlight and blood.

Working with the garden, Joseph has time to wonder how long Allister kept it, and what purposes the cage served prior to the end of the world.

A shambling corpse sways through the vines and flowers. At first Joseph sees an outline, a grey and vaguely human shape lumbering through the forest. The corpse makes its way past the vines and brush, languidly pushing through the vines that seem to be tugging at it like so many listless limbs. Its cheeks burst with rot and blooms alike. Joseph sees the black wound and the wilting yellow flower above it. It was not uncommon, perhaps poetically beautiful, for the creatures to get dirt and water stuck in their cuts, catching blossoms in their teeth and skin.

It moans slowly as it tries to push through the gaps in the iron cage. Its mangy grey hair is covered in bursts of pollen and tangled with fallen leaves, giving it the appearance of some dried druid mummy.

Joseph takes his sheers and continues trimming the branches and leaves, paying the walking corpse no mind. His aesthetic sense, a keen eye for decoration, developed rather quickly under Allister's custody. The silence of the new world allows for a clarity of mind, and Allister's blood invokes a sense of focus he never had before.

Allister liked her cage kept neat, her wild things proper and trimmed.

A thumb wriggles from between the gaps and lodges itself between his sheers. There is a wet squelch, but still the creature does not react.

Joseph hasn't been scared of them for a long time, not since Allister took him. In her care, he has done much to forget his past. He sometimes vaguely recalls parents and relatives, grey haired people opening Christmas presents and singing songs over the rims of their red plastic cups. But, for the most part, Allister's presence in his life has consumed and obliterated anything else he might be other than *hers*.

But mending the garden is a duty which forces him to confront how the world ended, at the hands of the shambling monsters inside.

Joseph knows that she hates them because of how she treats them. It makes for a stark contrast, her in a flowing red dress and beneath long red hair, clenching the throat of a piece of human wreckage caked in dirt and blood. She lifts them and tosses them by their necks into the garden with such force that sometimes they find themselves on branches and thorns.

Joseph suspects that her hatred has less to do with a grudge and more to do with what they represent to her. Not only are they a disruption of the natural order she once needed to survive, they are a fundamental defiance of the dignity with which Allister composes herself. There is something hauntingly aristocratic about her, the way she refers to her station and power in an accent that suggests that castles were never unfamiliar to her.

Seeing her with them, Joseph always remembers the old medieval wood carvings that he had seen in his textbooks, of skeleton figures taunting aristocracy during times of plague. Demonstrating that for all their wealth, and all their ornamentation, death would come nonetheless.

···

*She found him in an old department store, this much Joseph remembers.*

*He remembers the immediate fear, the feeling of cold she invoked in him. She was covered from head to toe in dark gauze, something that made her look like a black fiberglass mummy. Sunglasses prevented him from seeing her eyes, but he saw a spark of red shining through the bandages across her face. This, along with the way which she so mercilessly and quickly carved apart two walking corpses, was enough to send him running aimlessly through the store.*

*He tripped over mannequins, turned over tables, brushed aside dresses and shirts. He isn't sure when he stopped screaming, only that he somehow cornered* himself in an unlit changing room. He breathed heavily, putting his flashlight between his hands, prepared to strike her over the head if she burst through the changing room door.

But Joseph wasn't prepared for Allister to crawl through the abandoned air conditioning ducts. Unprepared for her to drop down on him with all the weight of a roaring storm.

Joseph remembers a pain unlike any other.

And a mocking, playful laugh as his world faded away.

But the surroundings he woke to were more disorienting than the throbbing ache in his skull.

The walls were made of stone, an open window revealing the night sky and allowing a cool breeze to waft in to lull his pulsing ache. A fire roared in the corner, painting the entire room in an orange-yellow light. There was a tapestry, adorned with beautiful pictures of a medieval scene he could not quite interpret. Banners ornamented with gold-laced patterns hung across the walls.

There were two seats. The one he was in, which he felt his hands and back steadfastly tied to, and the one she was in, a white, unmarked divan across which she laid in a relaxed, amused pose.

Her red dress was as ornate as the banners behind her, latticed with patterns of gold-leaf calligraphy. It ended below her knees and rose to just beneath her shoulders, where two scarlet straps held it against luminescent pale skin. Her hair was equally red, curled and large to frame her face.

Her smile would have been soft, were it not for the fangs which so neatly protruded from behind her scarlet lips.

In a different context, there would be no disputing her beauty.

But her eyes overshadowed the rest of her. They glowed brighter than the firelight, scarlet beams which cut right through him and into his mind's primal core. He trembled, sweating cold and breathing softly as her eyes ripped him apart. The color only served to complement her expression, that of a cat playing with its food. A child pulling apart an insect.

"Good evening, Joseph." Her accent was light, he guessed somewhere between Hungarian and French. He noticed her playing with a glass as she spoke, one hand sloshing the red contents and the other tracing the thin rim with a finger.

He could not yet speak, but the question rose up in his mind.

"Relax, dear." The way she said it suggested an age which her body did not show. "Even though the world ended, you thought to keep your driver's license and social security card with you…very thoughtful. Though I'd be careful." She smiled wider. "Someone might steal your credit card information."

The fire crackled.

"You know, I believe some thanks are in order, my dear boy." She motioned her arms around the room. "You see, I have plucked you from the dissolving world and placed you here in my castle. My meticulous home, built brick by brick by those who served me for centuries. It was important, tradition. The natural order. Both of which have seemed to have fallen out of fashion."

"Now?" She paused, soft amusement giving way to a snarl. "Now people just keep walking until their flesh falls off and their skeletons fall apart. With me, though, you will live...perhaps not forever, I have not yet decided. But you will live. Regardless."

She withdrew from the divan in a serpentine motion. In the flickering light of the fire she moved quickly, standing before him seemingly without ever having taken a step.

Her mouth opened wide, revealing that she had far more than two sharp fangs.

Her teeth were at his neck, her arms around his back. She gave no warmth, but embraced him with winter-coldness and death-stillness. His head became lighter and lighter, his sight dimmer amid the nauseating sucking sounds. His muscles went limp, and little by little the rational thoughts began to leave his brain, replaced with the half-dreams.

She moved away from him, brushing a frigid hand across a numb cheek.

"It was always a presumption of your species that the world would end with you," she whispered in his ear. "Now is the time of my species. Admittedly though, we cannot survive alone. We, however, are certainly more capable of surviving against this...other presence. They cannot run from us; they cannot rend us. They can hurt us, but we can hurt them back. It is much easier, dear Joseph, for me to rip a skull from its spine, than it is for you to even pull a trigger. My dear Joseph, I could snap your head off in an instant, you know?"

Somewhere in him, the dim shadow of fear sent a shockwave through his subconscious.

"But I will not do that." Now in the firelight her teeth seemed more playful than torturous. "No, I've grown rather fond of you. You will be useful...and you taste quite nice."

Something warm came to his lips and slid down the back of his throat.

It was not the last time she drank his blood.

•••

Despite her assurances that she would never kill him, Joseph never asks Allister questions if he can avoid it. He tries not to dwell on questions long, throwing himself into housework when he can. Dusting shelves, sweeping stone floors, and polishing suits of medieval armor is an easier task than remembering his past or thinking about his present.

There are no clocks or mirrors in this castle, no chance to wonder on how much time has passed. More importantly, he can be safe that he will never have to find out if his reflection is still in the mirror.

He thought once, while cleaning a wine glass, that he saw his reflection fading away. Leaving the room in unease, he persuaded himself that it had been merely a trick of the light. But the uncertainty sometimes slows him, and despite his best intentions he sometimes loses sleep thinking about what he might or might not be.

During the day, Allister is either asleep or she's "out."

Her sleep is too much like how it would be described in the stories. Resting in her dungeon, she is completely paralyzed for at least a day and a night, sometimes longer. He had once gone to check on her, finding her immobile and beautiful in her chamber. But the hate from her eyes forced him up the stairs, and the scars along his neck and back are a constant reminder of his unwelcome transgression.

Allister doesn't like to be watched while she's sleeping.

When she goes "out" she dresses the same as when they first met, thoroughly covered in black so that no part of her may be burnt by sunlight. When she remembers, she returns with food and water for him. More often, though, she returns with the creatures she regards as living mulch for her morbid garden.

However, sometimes she brings back something that scares him far more than the walking corpses. He dreads the days when she brings back crying, pitiful things with black hoods on their heads and thick ropes along their arms and legs.

He's learned to dampen his guilt, but struggles with a reflexive empathy. When Allister forces him to wield the knives himself, he does his best to make sure that they leave the earth with as quick a mercy as he can provide.

Joseph prefers this to when Allister does the killing herself. *Those* screams don't stop for hours. Sometimes days. Her laughs echo through the hallways, a macabre song of joy. In those screams, guilt consumes him and denies him sleep.

He wishes she would let at least *one* live, so that she might have another attendant to care to her castle. And he, perhaps pathetically, wishes for company. The days are lonely while Allister sleeps, and it is only occasionally that she pays any loving attention to him; and even in those moments he is aware that it is nothing but an urge to satisfy, a craving to fill for her. "Making love" to her can only *barely* be called that. She is so cold in her touch. So painful in her embrace.

She doesn't love him, though she knows that he loves her, his love inextricably tied to his fear. She is his protector, his captor. Occasionally, his lover.

Sometimes he wishes for love without fear.

...

He is tending to the garden when he hears the gates open and close. The birds, who normally sing to overwhelm the graveyard sounds of the garden, have a habit of growing still and quiet when Allister approaches. Joseph sets his watering can down and makes his way towards the gate, knowing that she will want him to help her with whatever she has brought back to the castle.

Allister stands in all of her black protection, in one hand holding a brown paper sack with bread sticking out. In the other, a rope, dragging a large, wriggling black sack with a pair of legs thrashing out of its end.

His stomach sinks.

He looks to Allister, waiting for some sort of response.

Her face hidden, she gives none.

Wordlessly, she leaves, dragging the whimpering sack behind her.

...

The screams don't start that night.

Or the next.

Joseph assumes that Allister silently killed her prisoner, or that she is quietly bleeding them to make them last.

He eats in his room, bringing a small piece of bread to his mouth when his door opens. Allister wears an unfamiliar expression in her eyes. Rather than her usual predatory playfulness, Joseph sees something that looks all too much like *sadness*.

She sits on the edge of his bed, looking away from him and down to the floor. For a moment he feels an impulse to lean over to her, to brush her hair aside and hold her until she tells him about whatever is bothering her. But memories of the force of her bite and the strength of her grip keep him paralyzed.

At last she sighs, turning her gaze from the floor to his own.

"My dear Joseph...I am going to go away again."

Already this is unnatural. Never once before has Allister seen fit to tell him what she was doing or where she was going.

"I need you to do something new for me."

"Of course," he answers.

"I need you to feed her, too."

He does not ask who, afraid that Allister will meet his question with her claws. For a moment, though, he hopes...hopes that she will lean her head on his shoulder and sigh.

But instead she turns away, the shadows of familiar cruelty working its way along a sharp, wry smile.

"Thank you, dear Joseph."

She rises and places a cold, dry kiss on his forehead.

•••

The woman sits behind a set of bars. Her bed is neat and simple, gently tucked and made with a sort of care that Joseph never thought Allister was capable of. There's a bucket in the corner, but the odor that comes from it is repressed by the rows of large candles on each side of the iron bars.

The woman is tall, with short brown hair that hangs behind the bottom of her neck. A narrow face, small nose, wide lips, brown eyes, and little ears.

Allister has evidently left the woman one of her dresses. It isn't red, but emerald green with silver lines that gleam in the light from the cell's narrow window.

When she sees him, she rushes to the bars and grabs them with white knuckles. She presses her face to the bars, and for a moment Joseph can't breathe.

"Please, please just tell me what's going on." Her voice trembles, a wind chime unsteady in a storm.

He can't respond. It's been so long since he's had a conversation, or any interaction at all. He realizes he's forgotten the sound of a human voice when they aren't screaming.

"Please, my name is Casey—"

"Hi, Casey."

She balks, blinking through her tears and removing her face from the bars.

"Umm... 'Hi.' Look, just, I've been kidnapped by someone. I'm not sure who. There's been this woman, she comes here but I can't quite remember what she does. She'll be there when I sleep-"

"That's Allister."

"Allister? Who's Allister?"

Joseph merely looks at her, unsure of what his response should be.

Casey runs her fingers through her brown hair and mutters something below her breath.

"Just...just tell me what she's doing to me."

For the first time in a long time, Joseph feels comfortable asking a question.

"What do you mean?"

"I mean..." Casey begins to pace her cell. She takes panicked breaths and pauses so she doesn't cry between words.

"I mean what is she *doing* to me? I don't... What is she making me *drink?*"

"What?" he asks in a cold, distant voice.

"What is that stuff she's giving me? It's salty, coppery, I swear to God it tastes like blood and I can't think straight. Please, just... Is she *drugging* me? Please, just please make her *stop!*"

Joseph slips her a bagged sandwich through the bars of the cell.

"I'll be back in a few hours with another one."

"No, please. Please!"

He stops and turns back with a weak, forced smile. "Try to relax. It will be different soon."

•••

When Allister returns a week later, five walking corpses trail behind her, tied at the wrists and trying in vain to chew each other's necks.

She kicks the shambling mass into her garden, watching them with burning red eyes as they disappear into the caged jungle.

"What do you intend to do with *her?*"

The words surprise him, how calm they came out. They surprise Allister too, because for a moment she turns from her cage and her mouth is open in a soft "o." She considers him, and he wonders what she sees. Her expression seems hurt. Or even afraid.

But then something sneaks back in, an animal hatred. A creeping wrath.

"You have always had good enough sense before, my dear Joseph. Why question me now?"

"You haven't killed her yet. Are you going to make *me* do it?"

"Ah." She laughs, turning away and back to the cage. "I see... You still consider yourself one of them. I suppose I cannot blame you for that self-delusion, desperate and pathetic though it is. No, no, Joseph. You have been quite different from the men and women that you kill for a long time now. Guilt is a fragment of weakness, and I suggest you excise it."

She doesn't look at Joseph as she passes him, a frigid breeze following behind.

"I'm not done."

He's terrified at the words, which come out of him as reflexively and unwillingly as everything else he's ever said and done for Allister.

"Then what exactly *are* you saying?"

"I don't want to—"

She's at his throat, slamming him by his neck against the iron bars of the cage. Her normal expression of bemused indifference is gone, replaced by a demonic countenance. He struggles for breath, his nails cutting and tearing desperately at her fingers.

With one hand she holds him steadily, while the other raises slowly, making sure that he can see her reaching for the cage door. It twists into a clenched fist before it's brought down on the cold iron.

*Bang! Bang!*

Tiny fingers probe his back.

"Did you truly believe for one instant that you were the first, Joseph? Did you believe that in my long life I have not had more servants than I can remember? Did you suppose that any *one* of them was *important* to me? 'Love' is nothing more than a human engine, something to get your hormones going so that your species can reproduce. It is all part of the same hubris which makes you so little compared to me. No...no, you are all just a means to an end. Just useful. *The moment you began loving me is the moment you became useless.* But one thing I never, ever have tolerated is competition."

She opens the cage door.

Joseph doesn't have enough time to regret what he's done.

...

Casey had come to know Joseph as well as she could in the week before. He was nervous but eager to speak, clearly desperate and starved for human contact. Despite the danger of her situation, she found that his soft smile was a minor comfort.

He told her everything about Allister. It was a confession for him, every word a stone lifted from his back. His story, about a monster who took him from the world, who he believed could kill him with a look, was already unbelievable before he told her exactly what Allister was.

At the revelation, Casey went cold. She crumbled against the wall of her cell, knees buckling beneath her.

She asked what he thought Allister would do with her.

He wouldn't tell her at first, refused to speak to her for days after she asked the question. When he finally did, she wept, *begged* Joseph to just let her go. To escape with her. In the end, he couldn't leave. Instead, he merely gave Casey a blank look, put a key into a cell door, and let it rest.

"*I wouldn't blame you if you left,*" was all he said.

She still hadn't believed all of what Joseph had said, not until she saw Allister lift a grown man with one hand and smile as he was eaten alive.

She had meant to say goodbye to Joseph, to reason with him and lead him away from the thing which had ensnared and ruined him. When the gate door opened, she hid in the bushes.

She now knows Joseph never exaggerated, that he never lied to her even once.

The memory of Joseph's screams as he was eaten alive keeps her motionless long after the sun rises. From the cage, the sweet smell of a recent death wafts with the fetid and feral smell that is by now all too familiar.

It's not a rational thought that propels her from her hiding place. What moves her instead is the sole image surfacing in an otherwise empty mind: a soft-smiling man being torn apart.

She finds the kitchen quickly enough. The sharpest thing there is a long butcher knife that feels heavy with destiny in her grip. For good measure, she runs her finger across the blade, watching her own blood slide down its shining surface.

She finds the dungeon next, exactly as Joseph described it.

Casey's steps echo into the blackness, thrumming against the wide stone and across the cold air. The knife feels lighter with each step she takes. She reaches the bottom and steps towards the grey stone coffin.

Allister looks up at her.

Joseph had said she could not move, but Casey hopes that's not true.

The look of anger in Allister's glowing red eyes certainly makes it *seem* like she's awake.

"Wake up, you bitch."

The look of hatred remains. But it is still.

Casey places her hand above Allister's face. No breath.

She takes the knife and cuts slowly across her palm. The blood burns, seeping from the thin wound and trickling down to Allister's face. Casey lets it pour, from the top of Allister's hair to every part of her dress. Then, pleased with herself as much as she can be, she lifts the knife above her head and clenches it with both hands.

There is a wet crunch, the splitting sounds of ribs and sinew. Blood bubbles up from Allister's chest. Casey knows the stories, and isn't sure if this is enough to kill this monster. She hopes not.

What's coming next will hurt *so much more*.

Casey runs her bleeding hand against the stone wall, leaving a red trail behind her. She moves slowly, letting the blood fall to the ground beneath her when she has no more walls to lean on. She lets it sink into the dirt, making it perfectly clear where she had been and where she was going.

She comes to the garden gate.

She's sure she will be fast enough, but the things inside are dangerous. There are plenty of them out in the world, and it wouldn't be a good idea to have any more of them free, here or anywhere else.

But she remembers Joseph left a door open for her.

She will return the favor.

She unlocks the gate and runs.
She'll leave Allister to her garden.
And everything in it.

**Author's Notes:** When I saw a call for "Monsters vs. Zombies" stories, I couldn't resist. I have to say, though, I'm not much a fan of zombies. To me they're either too gross, too nihilistic, or too banal. Not to say that there aren't good zombie stories, and I hope this is one of them.

When I had the idea of a vampire and their thrall surviving the zombie apocalypse, the idea of a story about abuse and Stockholm syndrome really took hold. Oddly enough, I came to like Allister, just like I wasn't supposed to. Keen readers will notice a vampire named Allister showing up a few times in my stories. One runs a bar beneath Los Angeles in the universe of my occult detectives, the Bartred family. Another is the sheriff of a vampire refugee town in a Weird Western I am working on. Hell, she shows up a little later in this collection too. I don't know if Allister got what she deserved here, or even if she deserved it.

# A Slower Way of Starving

CARRIE HATED BEING on delivery.

She liked working with her hands, kneading and tossing the dough so that it reminded her of the big parachute blankets she used to play with when all her friends were still alive.

The job at Pizza Meteora had been a blessing, an escape from a boring and painful apocalypse. The pizzeria was a living monument to better times, a pole to keep her tethered to a semblance of normalcy. It had been the place where she had gone for so many birthdays and a few dates too. She had gone there often enough on her bike for Carlo to know her "usual": Canadian bacon, jalapeño, and tomato. With its red, white, and green tablecloths and brown brick walls, Pizza Meteora had become a familiar and safe place when Glendale began eating itself.

Carrie had worked in the kitchen with Christina, a 36-year-old who had been the wife of the man who worked the kitchen before her. Christina was kind, patient, and caring, with callused fingers and a reassuring smile. Like Carrie, she had lost members of her family to the disease, and like Carrie, she was no longer able to turn on the radio and tune in to the lies from the men on the wall. And in the kitchen, they worked and talked, broaching every subject except the ones they had in common. Christina taught her how to toss the dough, how to make the sauce and lift with a paddle.

And then Carrie found her, crouched over a plastic bag of dough, stuffing her mouth full until Carrie gasped too loud. In that moment Christina was enormous, lumbering towards her with open hands. Hands that Carrie still sometimes felt around her throat when she closed her eyes.

The last place and person who made her feel like everything was normal were both gone. When she couldn't even open the kitchen door without crying, Carlo put her out on delivery duty. With Jessica.

"You're going to need to learn how to drive."

Jessica was 18, a former cheerleading captain who wanted to study medicine before the Eating Disease broke out. Before working at Pizza Meteora, Carrie knew Jessica from a distance. She was a tall, blonde girl with curly hair and a soft smile. She was everyone's friend, at every party, club meeting, and dance. Every boy in Carrie's class had a crush on Jessica, back when it seemed like crushes mattered.

"I won't need to drive. I'm going back to the kitchen."

This was the first time the two of them had been alone together. Carrie had been able to keep her distance from Jessica by staying in the kitchen. The older girl made Carrie uneasy with her cynicism, her lack of interest in the well-being of herself or others. Her executing Christina only solidified Carrie's unease.

"Uh-uh," Jessica responded without any derision or sarcasm, but no warmth either. "If you're *really* going back to the kitchen, then you need to learn to use *that*."

She took her eyes off the road and motioned to the gun strapped to Carrie's waist.

Carrie froze in her seat, every hair on her body alive and electric.

"That...no. No, I'll be okay."

"Uh-uh," Jessica responded, this time with sarcasm.

The ghost-grey winter sky hung over them, dark and dead tree limbs casting off brown leaves that whirled in the empty street. Chain-link fences sprouted up above the brown-yellow grass, tall two-story country houses falling apart under the weight of their emptiness and neglect. Some houses still had windows that weren't boarded, their occupants naively trusting their neighbors as their safety-net faith in humanity frayed daily.

But the traffic lights still turned red. Jessica stopped slowly and thrummed her fingers along the steering wheel. No one at the intersection, she began to mutter and curse. Carrie gritted her teeth, shifting the warm pizza carrier in her lap as she looked around.

"I think you can just run it," she ventured.

"Nope. I'm not getting another ticket."

The light turned from red to green and the car gently growled through the empty intersection. Jessica sighed and reached for the radio.

"No, please—" Carrie reached to stop her.

Jessica looked genuinely surprised, her mouth a confused and crooked sneer. It faded away into a knowing smile.

"Sure thing. We're almost there anyway."

All the cars along the suburban road were covered in thick layers of dust and soot, unmoved for months. Jessica slid the car along a sidewalk curb, in front of a pink-and-red-bricked house with a little yard of mostly black dirt and a dead magnolia tree.

"You're going to handle the food, okay? If you can't shoot a gun, that's all I can use you for."

Jessica didn't give her time to respond, swinging out of the car and into the cold winter air. Carrie stopped for a moment. The house had a white door with peeling paint. The windows were boarded up.

One deep breath.

Jessica opened the fence gate and waited for her to go through. Carrie didn't look at her, trying not to think about what would happen when she knocked on the door.

She shook her head and knocked three times, loudly.

The door ripped open. The hands went straight for her shoulders and shoved her backwards. The back of her head crashed into the concrete porch as her teeth came down on her tongue. She winced, the electric shock in her mouth riding the pain up the back of her neck and echoing in her head.

Jessica fired her gun, though Carrie wasn't sure at who.

"Hey!"

Jessica jumped over her, running into the house. Carrie stood up slowly, rubbing the back of her head to feel for blood. Nothing there. Just a bad fall. She was relieved until she heard another gunshot, one followed by the high-pitched screaming of a wounded man.

Carrie jumped through the open door, careening through hallways littered with takeout wrappers and stains. In what used to be a living room, Jessica stood with her pistol pointed at a weeping man. His skin was blotched in rashes and sweat, eyes pleading as one hand held a bleeding shoulder and the other reached for the open pizza box. He had already eaten two slices, reaching for another before Jessica lunged towards him.

The barrel of her gun jammed into the bullet wound, sending him screaming out in pain.

"Please!" the man yelled.

"Where's the money?"

"I-I was going to pay you... I'm just so hungry."

"Yeah. Where's the money?"

"By the door! By the door!"

Carrie turned around. The house was a dim mess, floor as littered as an animal's cage and walls that were rotting in brown-yellow splotches of humidity stains. The door was still open, a grey prism that shone light on a small counter beside it. Carrie walked forward, her eyes falling on a wadded twenty-dollar bill.

"H-he's not lying, Jessica. You can stop."

Talking made her sick, made her recognize that what was happening was real.

That it was normal.

Jessica nodded, putting away her gun and turning her back on the man. He looked at them nervously for one moment before turning back to his food. With bloody hands he plunged himself back into the box.

···

Jessica hadn't spoken since they left the house.

Carrie felt clammy and sick, pushing both hands against her stomach and imagining the juices churning in waves. It wasn't the first time she had seen someone with the Eating Disease, but she hated herself for beginning to think that it was no big deal.

"I used to write stories." Jessica smiled.

Carrie turned, surprised. Jessica's smile was easy and unburdened, the same smile she would probably give a worried friend. "Fiction, you know? Believability matters, even in the most outrageous story."

Carrie didn't respond.

"Is that why you don't like listening to the radio?"

"Umm...no. I just...I just couldn't handle the lies anymore." She patted her knees and leaned back in her seat. She closed her eyes and saw it. Her little sister, choking because she got so hungry she stopped chewing her food. A bright little face turning dark purple, the thrusts of their father's hands on her chest not being enough to dislodge the broken candy cane in her esophagus. Christina, stuffing raw dough and meats into her bleeding mouth in the back of the kitchen. And through it all, Jessica's cold and distant eyes. Eyes that were somewhere else, somewhere beyond the hunger and the wall.

"You lost people, huh? Before Christina, I mean."

Thinking about Christina brought it back. When each friend died, Carrie took them off her wall, confining their glossy smiles to a shoebox coffin in the back of her closet with other mementos of deaths that hurt. The routine deaths had been easy, the people who existed on her periphery in the school halls and who sat at far away tables in the cafeteria. Those were the sort of deaths she could go days without recognizing, only calmly realizing that a familiar face was gone days after the fact.

But the deaths that hurt were beginning to be too much, and her shoebox was getting too heavy to lift. And when Christina died there hadn't been a picture to put away. Only an empty kitchen and a roaring, ugly silence.

"I had another partner, before you started working at Meteora." Jessica moved the conversation along. "Ashley. We got tired of the radio, tired of the men from the wall telling us that everything was fine. So we made up stories. Whoever made up the best story got pizza, loser had to pay. I always won."

The road whirred beneath them.

"If you're gonna work with me-"

"I'm going back to the kitchen-"

"If you're going to work with me," Jessica spoke louder, "you're gonna have to start making up better stories. That, and you're going to need to learn how to shoot."

Jessica turned down a long road away from town.

"We-" Carrie started.

"Have time," Jessica said resolutely. She dipped her hand into a cup holder and pulled out a pager, something that Carrie had only seen before on *Seinfeld* reruns. "Carlo can ping me when we have an order. Until then"—she turned back to the road—"you're going to learn to shoot."

"I don't want to," Carrie said, fluttering resoluteness breaking under the thought of the gun in her hand.

"Doesn't matter. I'm not dying because you can't aim. But, I tell you what." She clicked her pause with her tongue against her teeth. "You hit the target today, I'll put in a good word with Carlo. I'll tell him you're getting over it. That you might be able to go back to the kitchen."

The dying houses fell away to an empty field. At the end of the road, the wall rested at a menacing distance. She'd been to it once before, with one of her more adventurous friends who only wanted to see it. It was tall, gunmetal grey, and patrolled by men who wore white hazmat suits. Locals were told that it was best to stay away from the wall, to simply let the men who patrolled it do their jobs. The occasional beat of assault rifles reminded them exactly why this was a good idea, as did the unburied corpses and the black crows with red strips between their beaks.

As they approached the wall, the billboards began to loom.

A smiling woman, her hands folded into a heart. *"Don't panic, just smile."*

Two men, money changing hands. *"What's good for the economy is good for you."*

Jessica turned the car away from the road, into the empty field. It jostled Carrie's innards, recalling the memory of the stinking house and the starving man inside. She put her hands over her mouth and nose, breathing slowly as the car sped along over the uneven dirt and grass. She closed her eyes and tried to think of something better. An old cartoon, the smell of the ocean.

The car stopped and Jessica stepped out, slamming the door behind her.

Carrie blinked.

"Get out."

Jessica's tone made it clear that it wasn't a fight that either of them really wanted to have.

She opened the door to yellow grass and cloudy skies. The air was warm and still, with languid humidity sitting heavy above the silence. There was a rusted barrel, bullet holes letting grey light shine through the other side.

"Did you teach your other partner to shoot here?"

"Ashley taught *me*."

Jessica went to the back of the trunk, pulling out an old pizza box and a roll of duct tape. Pizza Meteora's logo blared out from the drab world, a pepperoni pizza shooting across the cosmos in brilliant cartoon flames. She walked back, smiling before she clapped down hard on Carrie's shoulder.

"Pull out the gun. Feet apart."

Her side was heavy. She hadn't drawn the pistol and she already felt its weight in her wrists, the cold metal in her palms, and the recoil of the gun up her shoulder. She bit her lip, still tasting blood from her fall.

"Go on."

Carrie's left hand reached for her holster, trembling erratically as she choked between trembling breaths. The ground became water beneath her, shaking and wavering while her head got hotter and hotter.

"What the hell?" Jessica's voice came through from a faraway place, drawing her back to the empty field, pale winter sky and distant grey wall. Back to the hungry world where even ghosts didn't linger.

"No!" Carrie found herself screaming. She shook her head, tears blurring her sight as she ran back to the car and slammed the door behind her.

...

The men from the wall drove white cars at night. High-roofed, oval shaped things like classic Volkswagen Bugs with tinted windows and bright blue headlights. They would drive slowly through the suburb streets, sometimes stepping out of their cars to reveal their sterile beekeeper hazmat uniforms as they knocked on house doors. Sometimes the doors would be opened, they'd carry on a simple conversation with a wide-eyed citizen, and then a wave goodbye.

Other times there would be controlled fire on a dry lawn, rotten-sweet flames of dead flesh cracking and hissing with bubbles of fat. In the morning there would be a black skeleton and an empty house.

On Fridays, the men from the wall stopped at every door, honking their horns in warning as they approached each home with narrow envelopes. Three knocks on the door and they retreated to their cars, leaving the hungry world to look down on it from their wall.

Carrie opened her door to find the white envelope sitting on the porch, her name printed on it in neat type face. She took the envelope inside to the sparsely furnished house, opening it beneath the dull hum of the dining room light. It wasn't much, but it was what the men from the wall decided that she needed to survive. What she earned from her job.

She couldn't afford to leave Pizza Meteora. No one paid for electricity, gas, or water anymore, but there weren't safe jobs for teenagers either. The men from the wall pumped everything into the town that they could need. Everything but food. The men from the wall still made them buy food. It was the only way to keep everyone involved, to keep them working so that, for a few merciful hours, they wouldn't think about the dying place around them.

Carrie held the money in her hand, letting her fingers slide along its edges as she sighed.

There wasn't much left to want anymore. There wasn't a shirt she wanted, no concerts to get tickets for. There wasn't even anyone to get a gift for.

But the money still came.

She put her head in her hands, horrified at the prospect of walking up the same quiet stairs her sister used to slide down on Saturday mornings, of passing the bathroom where her dad shaved with an open door.

Their smiling faces and bright smiles were the only ones she couldn't bear to take off the wall.

•••

"Look." Jessica strummed her fingers on the steering wheel. "About yesterday–"

"I don't want to talk about it."

"You don't *have to*. Like I said," she cleared her throat, "I used to tell stories. About how this happened. What happened before, what'll happen after. If we can't listen to radio...you gotta tell me a story."

Carrie frowned.

"What about?"

Jessica motioned from the steering wheel to the wall, grey and looming in the distance.

"*Them. That.*" She sneered and flipped the wall off.

The wall was an ever-present obelisk at the edge of their reality. The days when the wall went up around Glendale were loud, full of crying and yelling. Gunfire broke the screaming, until finally it seemed as if the wall had always been there, that the men in the white beekeeper hazmat suits had patrolled the ins and outs of the town since time immemorial.

"I try not to think about them," Carrie curtly answered.

Jessica scoffed. "That's kinda pointless, don't you think? They're not going anywhere, and neither are you." She turned her eyes to the road. "The world is ending, and they're just dragging it out."

"You don't sound angry about it."

"Heh." Jessica smiled. "Like I say, why bother?"

"Well, *I'm* angry."

Jessica turned the car along an empty street.

"I'm angry because it's a lie," Carrie began. When she closed her mouth to bite her teeth together, she felt the breath behind her throat flutter. "The biggest fucking lie is that things will magically get better. That they're going to find a cure." Carrie smiled at the sound of the word.

"I'm angry because we all know damn well that there is only *one* cure. They may not know what causes it, but they know damn well what ends it. I'm angry because after New York went dark and it was pretty fucking clear they killed every goddamn person in Manhattan, they decided that it would be cheaper to keep us alive than pay for lead and shovels." She couldn't stop herself as tears of relief bubbled up with a low, hollow chuckle.

"You say the world *is ending*. You're naïve. The world *ended*. Just on the other side of that wall is a whole lot of hungry nothing. And they're just keeping us in here, delivering pizzas and pumping money into the town, because the only thing keeping this whole fucking thing together is the *delusion* that staying on this routine will let us idle comfortably to the end!"

Jessica blinked as Carrie burst out laughing. She held her ribs, aching at the alien, wild sound swelling up from just above her heaving stomach. She wiped the tears from her eyes, grinning.

"How was that?"

Jessica paused, turning back to a red light before the realization shattered on her face like an egg. She smiled. "You little shit. Pretty good. What were you, a drama geek?"

"Junior high. I was Ophelia."

"Well, hell. My little sister was a drama geek too." She paused for a moment before smiling again. "I mean…I like believability and all, but that was *too much*. Next time, try something that's a bit wilder of a lie. Good act, though."

Carrie beamed back. "The whole thing's an act. The whole thing is a lie. That's the only part that's true."

...

The first two houses had been routine. Carrie couldn't tell if the man at the first stop was sick or not. He was thin, jaundiced, and slicked with sweat. He nervously handed them the money as his eyes panned over to the street behind them. Jessica cussed and wiped her hands on the knees of her pants.

At the next house, a little girl no older than eight answered the door. She smiled, weary and relieved all at once with a suffering that seemed too old for her face. She motioned for the two of them to come inside with a dirty-nailed hand.

Carrie stepped forward before Jessica blocked her with an arm.

"No way," Jessica replied flatly.

The girl looked at her, her eyes welling up, bewildered and frightened.

"Please," her voice was brittle and small, "my mom is sick. We ordered but I don't know where the money is and she just fell asleep."

"Wake her up."

The child stared at her, incredulous and shocked. She turned to Carrie, who could only offer a sad smile and nod.

The girl didn't say anything, but turned around and walked down a hall littered with dirty paper napkins. Carrie peered after her, waiting to see or hear anything as she walked away.

From the end of the hallway came a wailing, a grating scream of someone bedridden and immobile with pain. The mother howled, crying out in mindless roars between pleas for food or death.

The girl came back to the door with glistening tears under her eyes, handing Jessica a folded twenty-dollar bill as Carrie handed her the pizza box. She opened it in the door, taking a spoon and smashing slices into a seeping, mushy sludge.

Carrie bent down.

"Let me help."

She took a slice in her hands as the girl blinked.

"It feels gross, but it's easier if you just mash it with your hands. She'll be able to swallow it a little easier that way."

"We don't have time."

Carrie turned around and Jessica was already walking towards the car.

"It'll just take a second–"

"It's not our job."

Carrie stopped. The girl looked up at her, emotionless and exhausted.

Carrie placed the slice back in the pizza box, turning back once to see the child furiously pounding her fists into the sauce and cheese as their car drove away.

Jessica was quiet for a full two minutes before Carrie finally spoke.

"It's tough growing up without parents," she ventured.

"It's *wishful thinking* growing up at fucking all," Jessica corrected, fury and frustration coming from her clenched teeth.

"You *cannot* slow down for the dying or you will fucking *join them!* And don't *ever* thinking about following someone into their house! Most of the hungry are just wasting away, but you remember what happened yesterday!? What'll probably happen again today!?"

Jessica slowed down and pulled up to a curb.

"Just get ready," she hissed.

The doors slammed shut and Carrie lifted the pizza carrier. The house was two stories and wooden, white paint stripping away to reveal worn, black bark. The lawn was ill-kept, children's toys and pink-tired bikes swallowed whole by yellowing weeds. Jessica's eyes fell on the toys and she held up a hand. She moved slowly, taking out her gun as she ascended the porch steps and knocked heavily on the door.

No one answered.

Jessica knocked again.

When there was no reply, she shook her head and turned away from the door.

"Don't like it, we're moving on." She walked past Carrie back to the car.

The door shattered wide open behind them.

In a flurry, the woman was on Carrie, her hot breath and brown teeth gnashing and yelling inches away from her face, her intent to kill and animal-hatred woven into every angle and every line around her eyes. Carrie couldn't scream, every thought and impulse in her focused on turning her tendons into iron as she fought with every ounce of strength she had to keep the woman away.

A popping sound split the earth.

The woman was no longer snapping her jaws, no longer clawing for Carrie's throat. Where her eyes had been there was now a dripping red mess, a tangy iron taste dribbling onto the sides of Carrie's lips.

She pushed the corpse off her. Her hands were shaking uncontrollably, her knees wobbling and buckling beneath her. She fell to the yellow weeds, vomiting and crying all at once.

She turned to Jessica, gun now hanging limply at her side, steam rising from its black barrel into the dull grey sky.

...

The pistol was heavy in Carrie's hands. She planted her feet firmly apart and took a deep breath to stop her hands from trembling. Jessica watched her impassively. Carrie lined up the sights, aiming for the pepperonis on the empty pizza box propped up against a brown-rusted barrel.

She fired once.

The bullet shot through the barrel, digging itself into the ground and shooting up clods of grey-black dirt.

"Try again." Jessica's voice broke the silence.

The trembling started, and Carrie could feel the hot stink of the sick woman's breath.

"Focus." Jessica's voice cut through the air.

She lined up the sights again.

The bullet shot through a pepperoni, tearing into the flaming pizza-meteor logo.

Carrie gasped. A smile broke across her face, and she turned back to Jessica.

Jessica only rolled her wrist.

"Again."

Carrie nodded. She raised the gun and wrapped her finger around the trigger and fired.

And kept firing until it felt normal.

...

When winter ended, Carrie didn't miss the kitchen. The idea of it seemed oppressive and dark, a small space to hide from the world until it came crashing through the walls in its final, inevitable death heave. She had learned to drive, and enjoyed being by herself in the long quiet between deliveries. In spring it was a pleasure to get out, to see the blue sky and the creeping return of green leaves and bursting flowers. Most jobs were routine, once word spread to the remaining survivors that she was just as ready to draw her gun as Jessica. Most of the time, seeing it in a holster was enough to keep people from attacking her. When it wasn't, usually pulling it out did the job.

When that didn't work, there was only one thing that did.

It was two months before Jessica called in sick.

It confirmed all their suspicions. Jessica had sounded desperate, manic as she ordered five large pizzas with whatever toppings they could find. Nothing mattered, she said, except that they were big.

Carlo asked if she was okay, tried to tell her that they'd missed her since she'd stopped coming to work.

"*JUST GET HERE!*" Carrie heard from the receiver.

Carlo shook his head and put the phone back.

"She's gone..." He sighed, waiting for Carrie to fill the quiet. When she didn't, he went back to the kitchen and talked to the kid in the back whose name she wasn't bothering to learn yet. Half an hour later, Carlo handed her two boxes with the flaming Pizza Meteora logo.

"Take this much, two large pizzas. If she gives you any trouble–"

"Yeah."

Jessica's house must have been the perfect place for parties. Two stories, painted blue and white, carefully maintained by a whole family that still looked forward to game nights and family dinners even as their kids got older and the world started to end. The once-beautiful yard had been swallowed by tall, spiny, verdant weeds.

Carrie closed the door behind her, throwing the bag over her shoulder and unholstering her gun.

She knocked on the door.

"Come in."

From behind the door, Jessica's voice was too happy, too cheerful and welcoming.

"No."

"I'm busy. I've got my hands full in here and I can't come to the door." From behind the door, Carrie couldn't hear any movement. But she knew Jessica, so she took a few steps to the side of the door and raised her gun before she spoke again.

"I'm not coming in the house, Jessica. That'd be really, *really* stupid."

She could hear Jessica moving just behind the door, the rapid thud of her footsteps as they pounded forward. She jumped back as the door flew open.

Jessica's curly hair was matted and feral, tangled in tumbleweed knots around a thin face. Her brown eyes were wild, gleaming off the kitchen knife arced above her head.

Carrie pulled the trigger of her gun and Jessica crumbled, dropping the knife and reaching her hands towards her chest as she crouched down. Carrie kept her gun drawn, approaching slowly to see exactly where the bullet had hit. Jessica cradled the spot just beneath her breasts, coughing violently as her lungs filled with gore.

Carrie clicked the pistol again.

Jessica thrust herself upward, barreling her head into Carrie's chest and knocking the gun out of her hands. She tore the carrier off her shoulder, sending Carrie crashing through a porch window. The glass exploded around her, cutting her arms and legs as she pulled her hands to cover her face.

The living room was littered with burger wrappers and take out bags from all the delivery places that knew better than to come back. Carrie brushed the refuse aside, realizing that Jessica had called Pizza Meteora as a last resort, the only remaining option to feed the hunger eating at her brain.

Through the broken window Carrie saw her, grabbing handfuls of dough and cheese as she tried to fit fistfuls into her mouth. She ripped apart the slices, letting the grease drip from her mouth like the gore from some freshly slaughtered prey. Between bites and breaths she coughed up blood, paying no attention to the seeping wound that poured faster and faster as she strained herself to chew and swallow.

Carrie launched herself forward.

Jessica fell from the porch, landing on the weeds and tumbling out towards the street. Splayed on the lawn, her eyes scanned the sky as she slowly heaved her chest. She breathed slowly, sweat and thick orange grease painting her face in a macabre funeral carnival.

Carrie stood slowly and looked around carefully.

She found the pistol, still on the porch next to the pizza carrier.

She turned back to Jessica, to the blue sky above her.

She walked forward and raised her gun, finding it was light in her hands.

**Author's Notes:** This story was written well before the COVID pandemic, for the now infamous pizza horror anthology. Though it was rejected from the anthology, it remains a favorite of mine and got enough good feedback from writers and editors I admire that I wanted to share it with readers rather than trunk the story.

At its core, this is a story about the horrors of a first job and delivery. There's a vulnerability in being a delivery driver. You have to get on the road, where all sorts of accidents could happen. Go knock on doors, and all sorts of people could be behind them. The story took on an apocalyptic setting once I thought about food delivery being part of this greater horror story of consumerism, this economic engine that doesn't see people for humans but instead dollars and mouths. This is the story of the end of the world as the bottom-line, with normalcy forced and imposed not to keep people calm, but to keep things going as long as possible.

# She Never Killed Spiders

THE WINTER CHILL snakes its way through the dying trees, drawing a thick fog from the forest floor and blanketing dry leaf-husks. Celeste hears them crunching under her cloth-thin shoes as she darts between skeletal trunks, unwary of red leering eyes or dripping teeth. Her lungs strain, ready to splinter their cage and shatter her ribs. Behind her, the rumblings of her pursuers are distant, but roaring nonetheless. She does not look back, heedless of the fog-hidden thorns that cut and tear her pants.

Celeste had seen the pictures of witch trials, the poor men and women who were shackled, whipped, stripped of their clothing and skin alike through the lash of barb and iron. While other folk mocked and laughed at the pictures that the travelers had brought to their village, praising God and licking their lips over the countenances of suffering, Celeste always felt sick. Even then she knew there was evil in the world, but did not see it in the faces of the supposed witches. It instead seeped up from the hungry eyes of the villagers, from the stony and resolute countenances of the prosecutors which held their hot irons to writhing flesh.

A root seems to spring up from the earth, catching her shoe.

She turns as she falls, trying as best she can to land on her back and save the journal she so tightly cradles in her arms. She bites her lip and moans quietly from the pain as her blood slides along her tongue. She does not scream. She *will not* scream. No scream she could give, no pain she could endure, would match the cruelty of the neighbors following distantly at her back.

She rises as quickly as she can, shaking as she scans the black shadows within the trees and brush. She knows the forests of Averoigne are haunted. *Everyone* knows, from the smallest child to the oldest widows, each spinning their too-near-truths about the demons that still reigned in the darkest parts of the forest. Until today there had been no force on earth which could have compelled Celeste to enter the forest.

A low growl comes from the brush. She stifles a yelp, veering away from the source and further into woods. The branches begin to overtake each other, folding and colliding into a dark ceiling that shields her from the cold, grey winter sky and what little light it gives. A lone bird caws into the distance, too big and too angry to be anything less than monstrous. Frost begins to tear at her as much as thorn, and she slowly becomes aware of the silence around her.

No birds. No monsters. No roaring men.

How much blood has she lost? How many cuts redly weep across her? She does not want to check, to slide her hands down her shins to count her wounds. There are monsters in these woods, the vampires and *loup-garous* who can smell blood from the darkest dins, burrows, and tunnels. She does not need to know how appetizing she may seem, or how vulnerable she truly is. She only needs to push forward, to push through the woods to whatever better, sunnier place exists on the other side.

A sound overtakes her nightmarish daydreams. A loud, almost wooden clicking; a sound not unlike thick tree branches twisting and breaking under heavy storms. First, only a few clicks come from somewhere within the deep forest. Then another. Too slowly she realizes they're barreling towards her. She runs, but her exhaustion has woven itself across her bone and sinew. Even breathing hurts, tearing her throat and forcing dark, warm fits of choking coughs.

Two sharp pains pierce her back.

She screams, but only shortly, as darkness overtakes her sight.

...

She wakes to find herself warm.

She cannot see, but she is warm. Moving her arms, she finds herself under thick, heavy covers. Pain hums calmly across her body, somehow soothing as a dim reminder that she has rested. She runs a hand through her hair to find it empty of twigs and leaves. She throws off the covers, and finds that her legs have been cleaned, dressed, and bound in white strips of cloth. No red peeks from beneath her bandages.

She is in a nightgown, a fine, silken thing that is comfortable and thin. She shivers as she looks around the room for something to wrap herself in.

Her eyes stop on the mirror. Celeste has only seldomly seen her reflection, on the surface of water and finer glass. Her face is still haggard, burdened with lines of worry that would need far more rest than she already had. Her fine, bright blonde hair cascades in curls down to her shoulders. Had someone brushed it? She touches her hand to the mirror and looks into her soft and scared blue eyes. How long had it been since she had seen herself so clearly? How long had she gone not having the comfort of her own scared smile looking back at her?

She sighs.

She's alive. Grateful for at least this one luxury.

She takes in greater details of the room: thick windowless stone walls, red rug beneath her feet, and a soft-burning candle on the nightstand next to her. She finds a thick, green shawl draped over a chair. She moves to reach for it, only to notice that her journal sits in the very same chair.

"It is an interesting work you have there."

The voice comes from beyond the open door, from a dark, lightless void. She stands frozen, looking into the empty doorway and hoping that she only imagined those words, that they are only an illusion welled up from stress and exhaustion.

"Come outside, my dear," the voice insists.

The voice is an echoing whisper, a low sliding of leaves in torrential wind. There is a shaking cadence to it, the melodic lure with which the serpent had tempted Eve.

Every instinct begs her to run. Her feet burn ready, her legs tighten and flex. But there are no windows, and there is no other door.

"I see," the voice responds. "It is no small wonder you are nervous. Please, get your rest, and I shall have your meal prepared when you are ready for it."

She hears no receding footsteps, no echoing footfalls.

After a time, Celeste moves back to the bed, shawl draped over her shoulders. She tries gathering her thoughts, attempting to reason and work through her situation. Her wounds having been treated and body cleaned; whoever had saved her, if she was truly saved, had taken great liberty with her person. But, as of yet, they have not done so in a way which placed her in danger. She feels no new sickness, only the pains which she had so recklessly earned in her run for life. And the owner of the voice, whoever they are, has opted to not force themselves on her.

After a matter of hours, the smell of warm bread and savory broth wafts into the room.

She has no way of telling how long it was since she last ate, and eventually hunger overtakes her caution.

She exits the room with a gasp, finding that the corridor, darkened only moments ago, is now lined with dimly burning torches. The ceiling is high above her, made of the same black stone as the walls of her room. Her thin slippers do protect her from the rough texture of the floor, though she has spent much of her life barefoot. She strains to listen, searching for some indication of where she is and what sort of trouble (if any) she is in. But only the crackling of the flames and the faint echo of wind answer her.

The journey down a spiral staircase is made faster by the smell of the meal.

Celeste emerges into a large dining room. A long, wooden table sits before her. In front of the closest seat, a bowl of a white creamy soup. She looks around again. No portraits hung, no family crest or banners either.

"Hello?" Celeste calls.

Nothing calls back in return.

She sits down, inhaling the smell cautiously. But it is too much, too rich for her to resist. She places the bowl to her lips, slurping it down in long, thick, hungry gulps. It is creamier than she is used to, a sort of luxury that she had only served and never tasted. The soup warms her from the inside, lulling through her stomach in gentle waves. Realizing she was hungrier than she could have guessed, she assails a loaf of bread, taking it into her mouth in tearing handfuls.

A low, sliding voice laughs.

The speaker sits on the far side of the table, having made a soundless entrance. Being seated, Celeste cannot tell even the approximate height of her host. They wear thick clothes and a hood, hiding their features within the darkness of the faintly illuminated room.

"I take it, then, that you were hungry?"

Celeste gulps, nodding. "Yes, thank you." She does not allow herself time to be afraid, having decided to keep the conversation moving so as to best protect herself.

"I am glad you are well. When I first found you...I confess, I was afraid you would die."

"Well...thank you, once more."

"You're quite welcome."

"How...how long was I asleep?"

The voice makes a long groan, as if thinking. "In all truth, I cannot say. I do not live with windows, and keep rather irregular hours. Every moment you were asleep, however, was one which I spent tending to you."

"What may I call you?"

Again, the voice thinks in its low grumbling. "Euredes Araignée. Yes, I often go by that."

"Monsieur Araignée," she continues, "I do not believe I can leave this place. I am Celeste Fortescue, and I beg your further protection."

"And, pray tell, would this have to do with the wonderful thing you have written?"

Her stomach falls. He *had* read the journal. But stranger still, she had not signed it. She wonders then how he knows she had penned it.

"I admit," he begins, "I could not tell at first what I was reading. In some parts it is a wonderful story, and then in others what I can only think to describe as"—he pauses again—"an *incantation*. How did you come up with such a marvelous thing?"

"My mother could read. She taught me to write."

"And, pray, is that why those brutes were chasing you? Why they screamed for your murder? Could it be that they did not like a woman writing such things?"

Celeste looks down at the table. "Monsieur, I do not believe they like a woman writing anything at all."

"Ah," is his only sad response.

"The world," Euredes Araignée speaks, "is often cruel to its greatest denizens." Before she can ask him what he means, he continues. "Your work shows you are a great talent. You should be proud of it. But again, I must ask..." He seems to clear his throat. "*Is it an incantation? Are you* a sorceress?"

She smiles. Despite the strangeness of her situation, despite the pain in her ribs, it hurts to laugh.

"Monsieur Araignée, to my knowledge, I have no such power. It is merely a story, with some tangents and poems scattered throughout."

"There is power in stories." His reply is grave and serious.

The quiet hangs over them for some time before he speaks again.

"Is there any other reason they so adamantly accused you of sorcery? Or was it merely because of your talent?"

She smiles sadly, recalling the story with a certain amount of fondness. "Two years ago, our village was invaded by spiders of all kinds. There were the small ones, which would work their way into hay and sheet while you slept. There were ones the size of apples that would build their webs in gardens and feast on bug and crop alike. And there were even ones the size of a grown man's chest... Ancient things, so large and so intelligent that the local priest proclaimed them to be the descendants of Lucifer himself. They were a terrifying, vicious blight, and in certain days it seemed as if every inch of our town was covered in a brown-black shifting curtain of legs.

"It was simple, but the knowledge had been lost to the village elders. My mother had taught me that peppermint repels spiders. While the rest of them took to the futile task of stomping them out, chasing their larger brethren into the woods where they could procreate further, I simply began spreading peppermint across our village. An easy cure to a difficult problem, but it worked. And I had their gratitude, until–"

"Say no more," Euredes Araignée interrupts. "The minds of men are fickle and malleable things. They only need to be told that there is a monster in the dark to believe it, and require the witnessing of only one strange thing to shake their faith and reason. A simple solution, as you say, but one with complicated consequences.

"You are a good soul, Mademoiselle Fortescue, but you could not have known your good deed would come with so undeserved a punishment."

"Might I petition your protection, then?"

"I would consider it my obligation and honor alike," Euredes Araignée replies. "However, I must ask for conditions."

Terror seizes her. The eyes of greedy men had fallen on her before, and in the darkness the eyes of Euredes Araignée are unseen.

"I ask that you continue writing, and you be willing to share what you write. Yours is a lovely talent, and I have so few new things to read. A second condition is that you stay away from the basements of this castle. You have probably guessed by now that I enjoy my privacy, and though I will grant you free rein of most of my home, I will still ask for my privacy. Another is that you tell me anything you want, and I will get it for you. And my final condition"—he pauses—"is that you tell me if and when you decide to depart. You are free to leave at any time, though I understand your reluctance to do so. I only ask that you depart this place as you abide in it, with my protection."

The conditions are suspiciously friendly, but she is in no position to disagree with them.

"Thank you, Monsieur Araignée. I will gladly accept these terms."

"Excellent." Araigneé's voice chimes musically from the darkness. "But you will forgive me if I add only one more condition."

"Certainly." She grits her teeth.

"You will call me Euredes, and, if you allow, I will call you Celeste. Let us not expend any energy on useless, cruel formalities."

"I see... Thank you, Euredes." She wants to smile, to be comfortable in her new conditions. Though Euredes has done nothing to harm her, the unusualness of her circumstances compels her to guarded caution.

For the rest of her dinner, Euredes only asks her questions. What was the name of her village? Had she written anything else? Was there one food she enjoyed over any other? He deftly redirects questions about himself. What was he doing in a windowless fortress? How had he come upon her? She resolves to press these issues further, when she becomes more knowledgeable of her surroundings and Euredes himself.

After hours of this friendly interrogation, Euredes suddenly stands from his chair. In the distance and darkness, she still cannot parse out the features of his face. Only his formidable stature and the length of his black coat make themselves visible.

"If you'll forgive me, I will excuse myself for the rest of the evening. You have complete freedom to explore the castle at your leisure, and please, content yourself to anything you find."

He bows slowly and withdraws into the darkness.

•••

Euredes becomes more forthcoming as they spend more time together.

He never comes close enough for Celeste to clearly see his face, but always stays just out of the full light of her lit candles. He still speaks in that same echoing whisper, and still makes great efforts to not talk about himself. She learns that he found her lying face down in the woods, two great welts rising from her back. He had undressed her, yes, and it was only when she pressed this issue that he revealed that he was a "monk of sorts."

"I have undressed and treated the human form many times, my dear Celeste." He had hissed this, as if frustrated and desperately ashamed all at once. "I understand your reservations, but I believed you close to death. I had to treat your wounds and clean you. I swear to you that it was a liberty I would not have taken otherwise."

That he is a "monk of sorts" explains the isolation, along with the interest in reading and writing. Euredes regularly inquires as to her writing, but refuses to discuss what she was already writing, insisting that she share her stories only when they are "complete and ready." She leaves stories, poems, and ruminations outside of her room at night, sometimes waking to loud, heavy clicking sounds which remind her of her blind, panicked run through the forest. When she opens her door in the morning, her drafts are stacked with additional notes, written in a precise and neat hand.

Euredes proves to be an ardent, though helpful critic: "Let your story breath more, focus more on setting and less on movement," he writes of the end of a story about a murdered god. "Make sure that you have a similar pattern of sounds in the middle of your lines," he responds to her poems.

Though still nervous, Celeste finds she looks forward to his insight, and writes with a greater speed and clarity than she ever mustered before.

She has yet to determine exactly how large Euredes' castle is, though she is certain there are at least four stories including the basements and (possible) sub-basements. She spends the time she is not writing or eating exploring the castle, and each day the mysteries of her current situation only thicken. She has already found a room full of gems, covered in dust and left to darkness and clutter, and a library, covered in spider webs so thick and profuse that at first she believed the room was filled with silken sheets. She wonders how much time Euredes spends in the library, and how he has read so many books with so little light.

She encounters spider webs all over the castle, creeping from corners and across ledges. But it is not until after the fourth day (she supposed, judging by how she slept in the lightless place) that she saw the creatures that were leaving them. She was combing through the library once more, reaching for a book she found with Euredes' name on it. She paused at the spine; Euredes' name was only a faint semi-gold mark that had faded with the wears of time. She reached for it before she saw eyes perched above the book.

She decided to let the spider keep its book, and only saw its eyes before she sprinted away. She has constantly heard them since that moment, and still finds their eyes peering out at her in curiosity. Celeste comes to believe that these are the sort of spiders common only to her region, intelligent and patient as foxes, content to watch and wise enough to not approach. She is fine with this. She did not lie to Euredes; she never did kill any spider or creature who crossed her path.

When she finds Euredes at the table where he presumably takes his meals (though she never witnesses him eat), she asks why the castle holds so many spiders.

Euredes responds by dismissing the question. "They may sense great good in you, Celeste. And because of this, they will not hurt you. They will, however, adore and follow you. Do not let it unsettle you."

"But *why are they here?*" Celeste presses again.

"They excel at trapping dangerous things."

Euredes does not comment any further on the issue.

A few weeks into her stay in the castle, she begins to notice something far more discomforting than spiders. She is exploring the castle once more, illuminating the kitchen with the low orange light of her candelabra, when she hears a shifting. She had thought Euredes gone, as she had not seen him for some time. She strains, attempting to overcome the silence and focus on the sound.

A dim roar.

The sound of something screaming from far away.

She follows these screams to a worn, wooden door. The sounds become quite clear, falling and rising in rhythms of agony. She reaches for the handle before remembering Euredes' conditions. The door slides open slightly. A man's voice pleads for the mercy of God.

Frightened, she runs from the door and attempts to convince herself that she only imagined the voice, only imagined those words begging for a release from hell and deliverance into the merciful arms of God.

But the sounds return, from behind almost every door leading to the basements below. She wonders if when Euredes explained he was a "monk of sorts" that he was beguiling her, belonging instead to the Satanic order rumored to thrive under the cover of Averoigne's darkness. The screams become constant as she learns to hear them over the presumed silence of the empty castle and the scuttle of spider legs. They become louder, more pronounced, awaking her from her sleep and tormenting her during her waking hours.

Celeste questions her soul. She has yet to find a Bible in Euredes' massive library, nor any indication that he was a religious man at all. She begins to wonder if she had accepted the conditions of the devil himself, or at the very least one of Lucifer's most ardent followers.

If there are souls down there, trapped and shackled to walls, do they not deserve her mercy? Celeste thinks of the religious men who chased her through the woods, who threatened to do unholy things to her before they burnt her alive. Thinking of this, she loses understanding of what "mercy" might be, and of who might deserve it.

But Euredes has promised to not harm her.

She writes her questions down, putting them between the lines of her poems and stories, hoping that he will no longer be able to avoid them.

But the stack outside her door only grows taller, and it seems that Euredes truly has left.

...

The clear screaming of a wounded man wakes her from sleep.

This sound is louder, more distinct than the muffled cries that extend from the basements below the castle.

"NO! PLEASE!"

She darts from her bed, throwing off the sheets and lighting her candle. She moves quietly, sliding her door open to creep slowly down the dark hallway. Around her the spider eyes gather, the falling of their many feet masking any sound she could make.

The voice shrieks above the crashing of furniture and the sound of rough fabric scraping against hard stone floors. From the second story she sees the man's torso, grabbing at the wall of an empty doorway with tear-wetted desperation. It is the first human face she has seen in a long time, something so pathetic that she almost cries out in sympathy.

He looks up at her, his mouth forming an astounded "O" before the darkness of the unlit basement sucks him in.

She walks toward the cries, down the stairs to the first story. Celeste finds the signs of an ongoing slaughter. In the wake of his struggle the man pulled rugs, overturned chairs. Dark stains of blood mark the floor, a grisly trail spreading in the small streaks of fingers and the porous wounds of split palms.

She arrives at the basement door.

She does not want to follow the dying man, pulled by unseen forces into the one area of the castle its master bade her to never visit. She screams, crying out for Euredes in the hopes that he would answer her from behind, but dreading she may hear it well up from below.

When she hears no reply, she steps through the threshold.

The stairs are taller and narrower than she imagined. Blood slaps against the soles of her shoes, with each step becoming hotter, darker, and wetter. She lifts up her light, steadying herself between each treacherous step.

When she finally catches sight of the basement floor, she does not know what to make of what she sees. For a moment she wonders if she is seeing a blanket of snow, a thin white surface which seems too smooth to be ice. She descends the last step, finding the white film to be dry, coming apart in strands with her touch.

The shrieks are right next to her, muffled through a thick binding gag.

The man is suspended from the wall, bound by the white substance around his neck. As he struggles, he seems to choke, coughing under his gag. His face darkens and his eyes widen in her light.

"Shh..."

She wades through the white film.

"I'll get you out of here, just steady yourself."

But his eyes are no longer focused on her. She turns away from him, towards the corner of the room where his frozen stare rested.

It is the height of the wall and covered in brilliant, shimmering scales. Its wide bottom oozes the white substance, and each of its eight legs ends in claws. Though none of its eyes have pupils, she can feel their weight falling on her.

She does not realize she is running until she is out of the basement; does not realize she is trying every door as she calls out for Euredes. She only hears the smacking of the legs below her, the wet splattering of innards on the floor. When she finds Euredes he is sitting limply at the same dinner table at which he had hosted her for so many days and nights.

"I wish to leave now!" she screams at him.

But he sits silently and impassively.

"Monsieur Araigneé!"

She moves to touch his shoulder.

The form beneath the black cloak is hard and wooden. She pushes the puppet to the floor, seeing a smooth, featureless face loll slightly to its side.

At each of its limbs are remnants of torn strings.

Celeste holds her mouth to cover her screams.

From behind her, Euredes speaks:

"Spiders are quite good at trapping harmful things...but perhaps you can spin webs of a different kind."

...

They are always easy to find.

They are the men who beat their chests, who shout the loudest in the taverns and threaten women with winks and promises of violence. They drink too quickly, talk too boastfully of conquests real and imagined.

She approaches them all, draped in a dark cloak with only a coil of red-blonde hair to highlight her smooth face.

She knows she is beautiful as she tells them her story. A mysterious beauty, speaking in honey-voiced words. She tells her story of a great and timeless thing of a monster in the woods, living in a windowless castle with a beautiful wife. A wife who will be all alone when the creature is slain, when its many treasures are taken. A wife who will be grateful for her rescue. And if she is not... Well, the castle is windowless, is it not?

They laugh and leer and, garbing her in slobbery words and slurring insults. But she merely walks away. They never follow her, always too scared to pursue something they cannot immediately understand.

And she smiles in the winter chill, beneath her black hood and red lips.

The men will come in the morning, after the beer has settled in their stomach and the story settled in their minds. They always do.

Riches and opportunities are irresistible to such dangerous things.

**Author's Notes:** Though Lovecraft is the far more famous of the original *Weird Tales* generation, I've always found his friend, Clark Ashton Smith, to be the superior writer. Smith is, somewhat puzzlingly, the least popular of the *Weird Tales* "big three" (the third being Conan the Barbarian creator Robert E. Howard). He has a gift for grafting poetry into his prose, forcing me to remark once, "Huh. So *that's* what the English language can do."

I set "She Never Killed Spiders" in Smith's fictional province of Averoigne, a place of werewolves, Satanic cults, vampires, and other monsters. I wanted to tell a story inspired by a love for classic fairy tales and fantasy stories, following the "young woman finds a mysterious caretaker" trope. A story like *Beauty and the Beast* or *Howl's Moving Castle*. The name of Euredes Araignée is unapologetically on the nose, but I don't speak French.

# Bestia

## SATURDAY, 11 PM

It was dawning on Khari that her boat may be too small.

That a similar sort of boat had killed her father.

The murky dark waters of the gulf heaved with the wind and rain, the choppy waves shifting the boat beneath her feet. The usual comforting vastness of the starry sky was masked by a heavy, pounding rain that made the air a screen of water.

*Focus, mija,* her father's voice whispered from her memories.

She didn't know what was coming, what was out there. The ocean was a big place and she supposed the thing could stand to take its time. In the cabin below she had everything she could bring. Every knife, every gun, and every makeshift javelin she found back on shore. She didn't think it would be enough to kill it, but it sure as shit wouldn't forget her.

The rain came down harder, pounding against her skin in cold, wet slaps in the near-absolute darkness. She leaned against one of her javelins and considered what to do next.

She put the javelin down on the floor and went to the chum bucket. Its stink burned her, repulsed her, but she dipped her hands in until her wrists were submerged in the red mass of gutted minnows and mackerel. She grabbed a fistful of wet and cold gore and tossed it out into the black water.

Then the sharks came.

## Thursday, 8 am

Khari Lopez hadn't expected to hear from her mother ever again. She was the only child, but their relationship bittered quickly in the wake of her father's death. Karina Lopez was a traditional sort of woman, or at the very least one who aspired to stereotypes. She fully embraced the cult of domesticity, the Catholic virtues of saint- and motherhood, not venturing beyond the boundaries of her home unless it was for an appointment to gossip at one of Sultana Beach's hair salons.

Sultana was a typical blink-and-you-miss-it Texas beach town between Galveston and Corpus. There had once been a small main street, full of seashell shops and seafood bars that had in time been taken back over by locals as tourists ceased stopping on their trips down the coast. Main Street had been repurposed for more practical businesses, an HEB, a Whataburger. There was still a fried seafood place and a bar, but they became the haunts of grizzled retirees and local schoolteachers blowing off steam. The teens (when they were still there) would go down the shore, after they snuck alcohol from their parents and whoever else they could, burning fires and giving in to their euphoria before the waves.

Coming home, the town seemed quieter than ever. The sidewalks were unkempt, sand from the beach piling up against brick walls and dark windows. Even the little bait shop/gas station/liquor store that Doña Matilda ran had a "closed" sign prominently displayed. There were no other parked cars, no people behind the dark windows.

Khari wondered if this was it, the last dying lurch of a town that couldn't convince its children to stay.

She wondered what would happen next. At first, she hadn't listened to her mother's voicemails, not even fathoming the possibility of returning her calls. Khari had chosen to take an athletic scholarship up north to get away from her mother and Sultana, trading warm Texas for the murky skies and airs of D. C. People sometimes asked her if she thought Northeasterners were "colder" than Texans, but Khari couldn't think of a human being alive more cold-blooded than her mother.

She spotted her mother's car pulled into the beach parking lot. Khari parked behind it and hesitated before stepping out. This was already close enough. She could still run away. There would be no shame in it.

She sighed, shutting her door and grabbing her bag.

The walk down the white-painted pier came with potent, tragic nostalgia. She remembered being a little girl, swinging between her parents' arms as they walked her down the pier, pointing at leaping fish and smiling at bearded fishermen. She remembered waking up early, coming out with a fishing pole and her father, who patiently taught her to bait a hook before he took her out on the water when she was old enough. She remembered going there alone, tears blinding her eyes as she ran away from her mother's curses and her father's empty office.

Juan's Seafood Shack hadn't changed. It was still a little, white-painted wooden ramshackle of a building, still plastic tables under red umbrellas with Coca-Cola logos and worn yard-furniture chairs. The tables were more crowded than the town had been, but before she could wonder about any of that, Khari saw her mother.

All her strength and breath left her standing there, mouth open and rasping.

It had been a little over a year and a half, but Karina looked like she had aged at least five. Her hair had become lined with curled gray tangles, her eyes sunken in and worn with lines. She paled somehow, and the new hue of her skin was imbued with the sickness that lurked just beneath it. Khari hadn't been ready for this.

This wasn't fair.

She didn't expect, after all this time and hate, to be in her mother's arms, to be crying against her chest softly in front of so many people. She wasn't ready for her mother's fingers running through her hair, for her soft whispers and gentle laughter.

"Carlita," she called her, the only one who ever did. The pet name that activated the fault lines of her emotions, calling to mind the "silly little *bestia*" that acted just like her father.

"Mom." The word was enough to calm her, to gently push herself away and sit down at a plastic chair. She shouldn't be embarrassed, though all of the patrons at their plastic tables knew her. She recognized all the faces that smiled sadly as they attempted to look away, people who, in any other circumstance, would be old childhood friends and mentors. She wiped away her tears, calmed her fluttering breaths, and looked back at her mother.

"Mom, when did you find out?"

Her mother frowned, looking for a way to say something hard.

"Not long after you left. About two weeks."

"Oh God."

*That's* why she called so much. *That's* why.

"I'm sorry," Khari whispered.

The breeze cut through them gently, lovingly.

"No...no, Carlita. *I'm* sorry." Karina waved over to the counter, shouting for two fish tacos and an order of fries.

Karina turned back to her daughter. "When your dad died, it was like I lost everything. I was crazy because I still had you. I was mean, crueler than any mother ever should be. You reminded me of him, and I took that out on you. It wasn't fair. And...even before that...I was too hard on you. You were more like him, less like me. The truth is, no one is ever ready to be a parent, *mija*. But I wish...that I could have been better to you. Our time apart, it's shown me that there's a lot left to do before I go."

Khari swallowed her tears again.

"I wanna start by making amends, Khari. I know you wanted to go visit your friends in San Antonio, but *please* feel free to stay with me for a while. I know it's hard, but—"

"Mom, yes, of course."

Karina smiled, exposing yellow and fragile teeth that only broke her daughter's heart more.

Mr. Juan delivered their order and winked at her.

"Good to see you back, *hija. Provecho.*"

And for the first time, Khari thought it was good to *be* back.

## Saturday, 11:30 pm

Khari had never seen so many sharks before, churning and thrashing under the water, sending up waves that thrust the little boat in wide, pendulous motions. They didn't make any sounds when they broke the surface of the water, only sent up flurries of blood and gore. Great whites, sand tigers, black as the water that hid them, glinting with shiny skin through the rain and ocean, kicking each other into a fratricidal frenzy.

She understood what would happen if she fell over, appreciating how stupid she was being.

*Brave's just the right kind of stupid.* One of her father's favorite sayings.

There was something important out here, something personal. She would wait as long as she needed to see it through.

She figured the thing needed more blood before it showed up.

She drew a pistol and fired into the water. The sound eclipsed the rain and the waves. The sharks bled through their wounds.

## Friday, 2 am

The beer went to her head faster than she thought it would.

Her mother had a bottle of wine, but Khari still didn't like wine. She gave her mother a sip of her IPA and laughed as her face puckered.

Khari and Karina stayed up late, laughing and remembering. For the first time, her mother was talking to her like she was a woman and not some frustrating little tomboy, or some horrible mistake.

And it was nice.

But it went to her head, sending her into a deep, drunken sleep that was shattered wide awake at 2 in the morning. She groaned, licking the sour dryness of her mouth and remembering where she was. Her old room was decorated with trophies. Swimming, gymnastics, javelin tossing. The golden plastic statues glinted in the silver moonlight that seeping through half-drawn blinds.

She was wide awake now, thirsty and vaguely nauseous.

As she descended the stairs, she heard the front door click open and slide shut.

"Mom?"

The living room was dark and empty.

She peered out the front window to see her mother dressed in slippers and a night-gown, walking down the empty sidewalk towards the beach.

"Jesus."

Khari put on her shoes and ran after her. Her clothes were sweaty after sleeping in them, but discomfort did not occur to her when she ran after her mother.

The air was warm and sticky. Her breathing was churning with her stomach, her mind leaving its buzzed fog with each hard step.

"Mom!"

Her mother didn't respond, moving forward with slow and uneven steps. Khari was worried now more than ever. Stage 4 melanoma, sleep walking. She would get hit by a car before the cancer killed her.

Khari hated herself for that thought.

"Mom!" She was closer now, clapping a hand on her mother's shoulder.

The face that turned around was all-too-familiar. It was the face of a woman that accused her of a being "a selfish little whore" while her father was missing; the face that said she was "an anchor that kept everyone down"; the face of someone who would laugh at her when she cried; the face of someone whose open palm stung just as bad as her words on the day they finally buried her father.

The eyes were enough to stun Khari, to send her reeling backwards as she fell.

Her mother's contempt washed over her for a half a minute before Karina Lopez looked away and continued walking down to the shore.

The town was silent around them. Khari debated going home, packing her stuff and leaving. If her mother was still that person, then there was nothing in Sultana for her. She should go now, before this became something else.

But she wasn't sure.

She had to be sure.

"Mom!" she called again, uselessly.

She followed her mother to the shore, where other people were waiting.

They were silhouettes on the shore, five or six of them. There was short and stout Doña Matilda, Mr. Juan, and a few more who walked in a line towards the ocean. They waded down to their knees, carrying something that hung low at their sides.

Her mother waded with them.

Khari waited quietly, stalking closer and closer.

She squinted, peering at the figures out in the water.

They had metal buckets, the sort her dad used for chum.

This wasn't the first shark fin she had seen off the coast, but her stomach fell as it approached her mother, cutting through the water like a black knife as it shot towards her. Khari opened her mouth to scream out, but her mother simply threw a handful of whatever was in her bucket towards the thing and it swam away.

Another came, and Doña Matilda flung a handful of something into the water. The shark stopped for a moment and swam away.

Whatever they were up to, it was incredibly stupid. Was this some weird bid to increase tourism? "Come see our tamed sharks"? She remembered stopping off at some swamp show outside Briarsville on a family vacation once, hugging her father tightly as some moron threw raw chicken at an alligator. Had her mother been inspired?

She marched closer to the shore, ready to say whatever was needed to bring them all in.

Then Mr. Juan removed a human arm from his bucket.

Khari screamed.

The people in the ocean screamed back.

**Friday, 10 am**

She was hiding in the old police station. The town really *was* abandoned. She'd left her cellphone at the house (*stupid*) and she hadn't yet found a working landline. Khari had no doubt her mother was waiting for her at home, waiting to cut her up and feed her to the sharks.

Khari had already killed Mr. Juan; she didn't want to kill her mother.

It happened in an abandoned bar. Mr. Juan had cornered her and started screaming that horrible, awful scream. It was the sort of sound that something makes when it roars underwater, a booming noise coming through in murky bubbles; like someone was playing telephone with his throat. She begged, pleaded, and cried for him to go away, for him to stop.

But he was much bigger than her, and made no sign he heard her.

He lunged at her.

She knew that if he pinned her, it would be over.

The broken-off pool stick went halfway through his neck before it stopped. He gurgled a little black-red blood up to his bottom lip. She couldn't see his eyes through the tears. Just the day before he'd called her *hija* and made her fish tacos. Years earlier, he would sneak her milkshakes, smiling sadly and knowingly as she sat at the end of the pier missing her father. A decade before, he had been her first childhood crush, with his wavy hair, wide shoulders, and thick black mustache.

It took too long for him to die, and Khari moved the pool stick to let him bleed out faster.

She couldn't believe that six people had killed the entire town. The police force had never been that big, but Sultana only really had 180 people on a good day. The police station was too clean and too empty to suggest any sort of chaos. No broken glass, files still in place. The locks had been electronic, and somehow disabled, so it was an easy matter to get her hands on a gun and bulletproof vest. While the vest was heavy and hurt her back, under any other circumstance she would have been grinning ear to ear. But she had just killed someone she knew, someone who wrote her a Christmas card each year.

She wasn't in a mood for smiling.

"It's out there, in the water."

Khari turned abruptly, pointing her gun straight into the chest of a short little old woman. Doña Matilda wore a scarf over her curly brown-black hair, her warm smile perverted by eyes that swallowed up the surrounding light in absolute blackness. She was *so* still. Khari wondered if she was even breathing.

The old woman took a step forward. She had babysat Khari growing up, even let her help out at the bait shop.

"Doña Matilda–"

"Khari," she answered coldly.

Khari put her feet apart and straightened her shoulder, resolved to shoot her if she came much closer. She meant to sound stern in her warning, but her voice broke.

"Stuh–Stay back!"

Doña Matilda laughed.

"Something *wonderful* is happening out in the water. All it needs is a little more. Just a *little* more. And it gives you *so much.*"

"Stay back, Doña–"

But the old woman's face changed again, the smile breaking into a scowl. She emitted a low, guttural growl and lunged forward. The gun went off, and a bullet planted itself firmly in Doña Matilda's stomach.

Khari ran to her, ready to administer whatever first aid she could. But as Doña Matilda died, she only laughed. With her dying breath, she made a curse: "You'll meet me on the water. Yes, you will." But the voice was not her own. It was a growl too awful to be human, too loud to come from a dying woman.

Khari made the sign of the cross and stood over her.

She'd have to do this again.

She'd have to get to her mother.

### Friday, 8 pm

The house was just as neat as when she left it earlier.

"Mom?" she called out, confidently.

She stepped into the living room.

"Mom, they're all dead. They wouldn't stop. I don't want to hurt you... Just let me stop."

Karina came from behind the kitchen door, a large butcher knife high above her head. Khari managed to kick her back, but her mother only recoiled faster, barreling into her daughter's chest and flinging her against a shelf lined with glasses and plates.

Her mother's face was contorted into a frenzied expression, the ravages of cancer replaced by the ravages of hunger and hate. Her face was more skeletal now with those black eyes, the same cold eyes that Mr. Juan and Doña Matilda and all the others had. She was stronger, too, strong enough to make this difficult for Khari.

Khari managed to plant a foot on her mother's stomach and pushed upward. Karina coughed up dark, sour-smelling blood. Khari winced, taking her mother's surprise to punch her just to the right of her nose. Karina cried out, screaming in a muddled roar.

Khari reached for her belt, withdrawing the nightstick she got from the police station.

### Saturday, 1 am

When her mother stirred, her eyes were brown and wide.

"*Mija?*" she asked meekly, confused and desperate.

The handcuffs were doing the trick, the ropes were doing the rest. Karina's hands were behind her, her arms and legs tied steadfastly to the chair she was in. Khari had treated her wounds as best she could.

"Are you thirsty, Mom?"

Her mother nodded sadly, desperately.

Khari moved closer, lifting a plastic cup of ice and water to her mother's lips.

She took a slow, weak sip. Then she bit into Khari's hand.

Fire shot up Khari's wrist as she screamed in surprise and shock. The blood welled as she desperately tied to patch up her hand with a paper towel. That's when she noticed the cruel, gurgling laughter coming from her mother's mouth.

"You were always a gullible little *slut*, Khari."

Khari looked back through her tears, seeing that the blackness had come back to swallow up her mother's eyes.

"So, this is how it's going to be, then?"

The thing in her mother laughed, loud enough to shake the walls and force Khari to move her hands to her ears. Khari closed her eyes. When she opened them, the expression on her mother's face was one of absolute terror, the white in her eyes coming back into full view.

"Carlita... I am so sorry... I just want your father back. And it only needs a little more."

"What needs a little more, Mom?"

"COME OUT ON THE WATER," the gurgling cruel voice hissed. "GIVE *ME* MORE, AND I'LL GIVE YOU *EVERYTHING*."

"More *what?*" Khari hissed back.

The thing smiled at her now, amused at her ignorance.

"What do you *think?*"

It threw her mother's head back and laughed, howling above Khari's pleading questions. After her throat had gone hoarse and ragged, she gave up and locked the thing in a closet.

As she closed the door behind her, she could still hear it laughing.

## Sunday, 3:30 am

The waves were subsiding, slowing down to a sloshing lull. The storm was dying down as the shark corpses around the boat moved slowly with the gentle waves. Khari wondered if her boat was floating on more water or more blood, or if that even mattered in the scheme of things. The air was miasmic and acrid as the gulls flew down to join the remaining sharks in feasting on the gore.

Biology was catching up with her. Adrenaline could only take her so far. She had packed every weapon she could think of, but not one thermos of coffee.

She turned around to go down to the cabin and he was there.

She dropped the javelin she was leaning against, struggling for breath. Her mind reeled, thoughts turning from words to guttural sounds of shock. He was wearing his overalls, his beer belly poking out gently from beneath his wide shoulders. He didn't have any sleeves, and in the light of the boat she could see the tattoos that used to fascinate her so much when she was just a baby. The tattoos that he got when he was in the coast guard, to commemorate the day he lost a friend while rescuing some fishermen off the coast of Nicaragua.

He smiled at her with green eyes and scratched the scraggly beard that her mother had always hated.

He winked at her, playfully.

"*Mija,*" he said gently, lovingly.

The storm was dead around them. Everything faded away, the gulls, the churning of the sharks.

She couldn't say anything in return.

He laughed. "What, *nothing?*"

"How?" The word sounded pathetic coming out of her mouth.

He beamed, glowing in the artificial light of the boat.

"There is something *wonderful* out here in the water, Carlita. Something beautiful. And all it needs is a *little more*." He spread his arms, motioning his hands to welcome her for an embrace.

She desperately wanted him to hold her; with every ounce of her being she wanted it to be true. But there was one word in that, only one word, that told her that it wasn't. She stood firm, resolute, waiting for him to continue.

He looked confused, feigning impatience with a snort and a smile.

"What do I have to do, beg? Come on, give your dad a hug. I've missed you so much, *mija!*"

"You're not him." She meant to sound cold, but it came out sad.

"What?" he asked, confused and hurt.

"He never called me 'Carlita.' Mom called me 'Carlita,' after him. Her way of calling me a boy. That used to hurt my feelings, so he never called me that."

She bared her teeth now, rage swelling up to replace the desperate sadness.

"Whatever you are, *fuck you!*" She reached for her pistol and pointed it at the thing's chest.

The thing's arms, covered in the tattoos of her father's skin, fell limp to its sides. Its eyes went blank, black and empty. Its expression melted into indifference. For long seconds it stood still as Khari tensed to fire another shot. Then, the rain began again.

The wind picked up, rocking her little boat. In the sudden crack of lightning, she saw it walk away, off the bow.

"No, wait–"

There was a meager plop on the surface, the churning waves quickly covering up any trace it had left. She reached for a flashlight, peering out for any sign of it. The water was red-black, flaked with white foam and pepper-marked with rain. Dark forms floated just beneath the surface, the steam of blood kicking up from below.

Two crimson circles reflected beneath a cloud of blood.

A long, rough arm shot out of the ocean and grabbed her shoulder, its rough skin cutting into her own. She twisted, taking the pistol and firing straight into one of the glowing red eyes. But it was too late, and the arm pulled her down her into the water below.

She was blind. She couldn't breathe.

She broke for the surface, gasping and panting. She had left the boat's ladder down and saw the glint of its metal. She kicked, hoping there was enough blood in the water, bitter and metallic in her mouth, to keep the sharks busy.

She didn't remember climbing the ladder, couldn't tell how close they got to her.

She reached for the closest thing she could find, the javelin she had dropped when the thing in her father's form had shocked her.

It leapt from the water.

It was massive, the size of her boat and more, sending her falling backwards as the boat shifted with its wake. The salt and blood sprayed into her mouth, sucked down her into her lungs and sending her into a coughing fit. Her chest heaved and hurt as she crawled forward, tightening her grip on the javelin spear as much as she could. She stood cautiously, the world shifting once more.

"Come on then, you bastard!"

The thing broke the water again. Directly in the light of the boat she saw a mass of arms and fins, a pointed body, and a mouth of thousands of glinting teeth opened wide as a door.

The javelin went through the open mouth, past the rows of jagged teeth and deep into the tangle of flesh.

There was a wet slice, a loud splash, another long moment of the ocean heaving beneath her.

Slowly, the storm cleared.

As the sun finally rose, she couldn't stop laughing.

**Sunday, 8 a.m.**

She opened the door to her mother's house.

"Mamá, it's over."

The house was still a mess from their fight, broken plates and glass covering the floor in jagged chips. She knew her mother would be relieved, that finally she would be able and willing to explain what had happened and why.

But the chair wasn't where Khari had left it.

There was an animal growl as something rammed itself against her back. Khari turned to see her mother, hands still bound but legs free, arched over by the chair. The handcuffs had held, but Khari was always shit for knots.

Khari swept her leg under her mother's feet, tripping her quickly and definitively.

On the floor, the thing in Karina's body yowled in anger and humiliation.

"You think you're a clever little bitch, don't you, Khari? Your *mother* doesn't think that! She thinks you're a stupid little girl, one who always wanted to be like a boy! She's said it before and you know it's true!"

"Shut up."

"She thinks you're a slut because you couldn't have a boy otherwise! Your mother *hates* you, Khari!"

"Why don't you let *her* say that, then?"

The room fell silent. Outside, the seagulls cawed, the waves sang gently.

"I'm not in the habit of giving back things I take."

"Oh."

So that was it, then.

"You're a little fool, Khari. You've only killed one *aspect*. I am *everywhere*." It smiled now, leering at her with her mother's face. "The waters are so big and there is so much coastline. So many desperate people and I can *smell* their heartbreak, their sadness. Just like I can smell *yours*!"

"Oh?" A smile spread wide across her face.

### Sunday, 8 pm

She packed as many coolers as she could into the back of her mother's car, filling them with all the food she could grab. She then went to the shops, filling the rest of the car with every piece of clothing she liked, that her mother would have liked. There was no one in the shops anymore, no one to mind or be hurt by a little robbery.

She buried the bodies on the beach, little popsicle-stick crosses that were about as much as she could manage. She said some prayers, though she wasn't sure they would be heard.

She stared at the gulf longer than she thought she would, at the ocean that had taken her father.

The ocean had taken so much.

Night fell, and it was time to go. There was nothing in Sultana anymore.

Someone might come looking for her, but she didn't care.

There was something big out there, something personal.

She slipped into the driver's side door, opened a bag of Cheetos, and turned to the passenger seat.

"Hungry?"

The thing with her mother's face snorted in contempt. She had bound it tightly with handcuffs, chains, and ropes.

"You're a brave girl, aren't you?"

Khari held a chip to her mother's lips.

"Brave's just the right kind of stupid."

The monster was silent for a moment. Then, admitting defeat, opened its mouth.

After a few minutes of feeding it, Khari turned from the monster and started the car.

"Where are you taking me?" it asked.

Khari shook her head. "I'm not *taking* you anywhere. You said you were out there, so I'm coming to you. Just tell me where."

The thing laughed. "There are so many bodies. So many aspects."

"Then just tell me where to start." She said it without resentment, as if it were only a matter of fact.

The thing pondered for a moment before smiling cruelly.

"West. California. Big Sur."

Khari nodded, turning the radio up a little. They had gotten through one song before the thing chimed in. "You can't stop me. You can't even begin to *know* me, to know *what I am*."

"California, you said? I'd say we have more than enough time to get to know each other."

She turned up the stereo and tuned out its taunts with "Me and Bobby McGee," only looking back once at the empty main street as it faded to darkness.

**Author's Notes:** If you've never heard it, "Me and Bobby McGee" by Kris Kristofferson is about the saddest, most beautiful song. It's one that always gets me a little close to tears, because it just seems like the story is over. Definitively.

The Texas Coast is a weird place. Corpus Christi is a tourist town, but without the level of tourism you'd see in a Florida or a California. South

Padre is a state park where you can camp on the sand and sleep by the dull roar of blue-brown waves. Galveston, of course, is its own little world-island. But there are places between, small towns where people make their living fishing and selling bait. Places that sometimes seem like seaside ghost towns, where worn paint and fried food just settle above murky green water.

I don't know when I first got the "*Jaws* meets *It*" thought, but I had to write it. Khari was supposed to come back too. There was something waiting for her in California, on a jagged coastline beneath a cold pine forest. But so far, I haven't told that story.

# With All Her Troubles Behind Her

## I

PAN PEERED THROUGH the sights of her rifle.

The boy she rested her bead on couldn't have been older than seventeen. Scraggly, ragged brown hair and a scowling mouth full of half-teeth already ruined by tobacco. He paced slowly at the opening of the mine, swatting his gloved hands against his pants and periodically spitting out something black and viscous. The men around him had the blackness pouring out of the corners of their eyes like charcoal tears, streaks going down their faces and across their lips. It seeped from their ears and noses, from every exposed orifice of their bodies as diseased war paint.

There was no hope for them, and only one cure.

She sighed, shook her head, and put the carbine across her lap.

The winters were colder in Utah than San Francisco, and the Rockies had been one hell of a hike. A train ride to Salt Lake, a three-day horse ride, and a day's hike. For what? She wasn't a *hero*. At least, not one that she would want on *her* side anyway. This didn't concern her, she shouldn't have to kill a bunch of men who, until a month ago, had been churchgoing, God-fearing innocent husbands and sons. She shouldn't have to play the sinner again.

She cursed and picked up her rifle again.

The wind blew across the pines, batting her face in cold, searing snow. She lined her sights on the boy. He'd be the first, but he wouldn't be the last. She wanted to say a prayer, to say *something*.

But she didn't believe in God, just *gods*.

And they weren't worth praying to.

She squeezed the trigger.

"I'm so sorry."

The gun bucked and the boy's head splintered open. He fell to the ground slowly, his knees folding in as his neck wobbled under the shifting wet weight. A roar went out from the others. She reloaded her weapon quickly, even though they would be slow to find her, weighed down by the snow and blinded by the pestilence that had overtaken them. She waited for another, a balding man with a scraggy grey beard. She fired into his stomach and he fell to the snow as dark, infected blood bled through his fingers. A third, a tall man with onyx black hair and shoulders as wide as the world, grunted and growled as he recognized the glint of her rifle.

She gritted her teeth, standing so that she could run towards the man, matching his careening momentum with her own. Her hands went around the barrel of her gun, turning it so that she could launch the stock into his jaw. There was an ugly snapping sound, a twig splintering into shards. The man fell back, and before he could stand she put a bullet right into the center of his forehead.

*Crack.*

The birds scattered, crying out in panic. The winter was wild around her, masking her sight in a flurry of snow as the wind rose furiously against her.

She squinted through the storm. Two dark silhouettes made their way through the flurries, circling her like angry, lonely animals. As the wind calmed, she could see their glinting, barred teeth. They came close enough to see, hissing and moaning as the black pestilence bubbled from behind their teeth. They were beyond speaking now, beyond reasoning. Their bodies did not belong to them. Their minds were long gone.

They moved slowly, waiting for her to respond. Their eyes were red with burst blood vessels, probably leaving them nearly blind.

Pan shook her head, reaching for the knife sheathed just outside her coat.

"Come on then."

A man got near her, a short fat man who probably smiled at his grandchildren and told his wife dirty jokes. Maybe he was a blacksmith, maybe a tailor. Whatever he had been, he didn't deserve this. He lunged at her and the knife went into his neck with little resistance. Just a wet slip, as if it was meant for him.

The other man ran at her, and the knife pierced his stomach before digging across his chest.

The black gore cascaded down on her.

She panted, looking around one more time. There were no signs of a fire, no coals or pots to cook with. They didn't need to eat, not since what was down in that mine took over them. Pan resisted the urge to cry. She was doing her part, doing what was right, even if it didn't look that way.

She wiped the snow away from her face.

The mountain air howled. The entrance to the mine was wide and dark. Something drafted up from within, charging the air with all the anger and cold of a wrathful, hungry panther.

She slung her single-shot rifle over her shoulder and sheathed her knife. There was no telling how many more dead men there would be before this was over.

Her hand came to her chest, where a little box just big enough to hold one cigarette rested along a twine ribbon. Reminding herself that the box was there reassured her.

The odds were already stacked against her.

It wasn't just a bunch of diseased miners she needed to worry most about, after all.

Pan sighed and let her hand slip from the box and the thin cord that kept it around her neck, stepping into the mine resolute to finish her work.

## II

"I don't understand why you're here. Or even how you knew how to find me."

The woman in Pan's office was petite, no older than 17. She was mousey, with a narrow nose and a downward eye which told Pan that she was not someone who was comfortable here. Her flowery, too-heavy dress was no fit for a San Francisco summer, and outside the growing city was heaving with a sultry, humid fog.

Pan's office didn't help. A plain, wooden room with a wide window facing towards the bay which captured all the moisture and heat the breeze could bring. It rested in a two-story brownstone, with grey-brown wooden floors and empty walls. Only Pan's desk and one single bookshelf were visible in the yellow-blue light of an oceanside day.

"I'd heard that there might be bounty hunters in San Francisco."

Her accent was atrocious and unidentifiable. But people often said that about *Pan's* accent, who still had trouble with American pronunciation even after all these years.

"Yes, ma'am, that's true." Pan lifted her boots onto her desk. "You can't sling shit without hitting a bounty hunter here. Gold dries up and what's a boy to do? There ain't much gold left, but plenty of bodies. Real good money to be made in bodies, let me tell you."

"But I–" The woman paused, twiddling her thumbs and looking down to the floor.

"You what, sweetheart?"

The woman stopped, giving Pan a sour look.

"Abigail."

Pan laughed. "All right, you *what*, Abigail?"

Abigail resumed her sad, reluctant look. "I heard about *you*. About a problem you solved outside of Carson City."

Pan narrowed her eyes. This wasn't a normal job then. She was perfectly content killing criminals. Your murderers, rapists, hell, she'd even killed her fair share of spies in her life. But that wasn't what this was going to be. This would hit closer to home.

She opened her desk drawer. The whiskey flask was a tall one, so she heaved it up onto her desk and dug for two glasses. She poured a fist of rye into the first glass and then motioned to Abigail, who shook her head and crossed her hands.

Pan took a sip, letting the slow burn rest just behind the back of her lip.

"Yeah...that was a railroad man." Pan sat down and thought about Carson, about the dusty town surrounded by smooth, dry mountains. "He came back from some expedition to Egypt with something he thought was a genie. Something he thought he could use. But it wasn't a genie. And it used *him*. So."

Pan put down her glass and looked at Abigail head on.

"What am I dealing with?"

And Abigail told her story. The story of a mining town in northern Utah, about a mine drying up and a group of men who were desperate to feed their families. Men who dug deeper and deeper, men who sometimes stayed up in the mountains for weeks and wouldn't come down until they had *something* they could sell.

The story of the day they all finally *did* come back.

Men who had loved their families were suddenly cruel, men with newly evil eyes who came at night to rob their own sons from their beds. Men who at first hit, and then tortured the ones they love. And then there were the women, the women who escaped that dead mining town, who left the men to their mountain in the hopes that they could find someone who could help.

The story of a girl named Abigail, who after hearing stories in Carson about a "young woman bounty hunter" who dealt in "spooky shit" in San Francisco, came all this way just to see her.

Pan nodded solemnly, looking out the window and onto the ever-growing city below. Her faded reflection didn't betray her secrets. Her tan, smooth skin was as olive-colored as the day she was born, without blemish or mark. Her fiery red hair was cut short, her deep brown eyes sad and dark.

"How old are you, Abigail?" Pan asked.

"Sixteen."

Pan snorted, wondering what would happen if she revealed her age to the young woman. Would she leave, offended and angry? Would she scream and run away, screaming "witch" or "demon?" Or would she just sit there in silent disbelief until Pan abandoned the subject?

Pan would leave it. The poor girl had already been through enough.

"Your husband." she thought of how to delicately ask before giving up. These stories were hard ones, no point trying change that..

"Was your husband one of the men who...*changed?*"

"Yes, ma'am," was all she said.

Pan nodded, deciding not to say anything further.

"I can help you." She paused, taking a draught of rye that slid down her throat in thick, playful burning streams. "But I have to tell you, there's no saving them."

"What?"

"I hate to say it." Pan stood from her desk again, leaning over it so she could look Abigail squarely in the eyes. "But if they've got what I think they've got, there's no getting them back. They died up on that mountain. What came down..." She tried to think of a delicate way of saying what came next. "What came down wasn't them."

"Then how are you going to help?" Abigail's face was angry, desperate and confused. Poor girl.

Pan stared at her, waiting for Abigail to figure it out herself. When she did, her eyes widened and her mouth formed a listless "O."

"Do you think you could point out where they are on a map for me?" Pan let a little affection back into her voice.

Abigail nodded, and Pan unfurled a map on her desk. It was marked with x's and lines, traces of one-woman massacres across the continental United States. For a moment, she was wrecked with pains of nausea and sadness.

She swallowed her rye and grunted, handing Abigail a pen.

A little circle in the mountains of northern Utah.

A little circle surrounding those poor, damned bastards.

### III

Pan wondered if she had already killed Abigail's husband. A young girl like that could have been married to any one of those men. People that far away from civilization tended to not care about things like age. Love was love and they would take it where they could get it, even when it wasn't love at all.

The mine was dark and frigid, colder than the air above. Her heavy hide coat was weighing her down, slowing her movement and making loud whooshing sounds with each stride. This sort of work was easier in the summer. Her mind drifted back to the last time.

To Carson City.

She had stopped keeping track of how many people she had killed. She probably stopped counting after she turned fifty. Hundreds of years later, the number became even more irrelevant. But it didn't stop hurting each time. If anything, her immortality made life seem *more* precious.

She was always amazed at what people were willing to throw it away for.

Footsteps plodded ahead of her.

She unslung her rifle.

He was a big boy, almost seven feet tall. He growled, throwing his head around like a bull as he quivered with blind, animal rage. If he could get his hands on her, he would rip her to shreds.

Pan pulled her trigger and hit him squarely in the chest. He fell, and before he could get back up she planted a bullet between his eyes.

Her ears were ringing with her rifle's echo. She swore, not sure if she could handle another shot without going deaf. Further down in the mine, an angry, shocked scream rose from a gurgling throat. She should have brought a sword. Swords were good weapons for this sort of thing, long enough to give a bit of range and quiet enough to not go deaf. But all she had was her rifle, a revolver, and a knife.

She would've thought it would been easier by now, that guns would make it faster than spears and swords. But blood was blood, no matter how it was spilled. She'd been doing her work for centuries, first with iron, then with steel, and now with gunpowder. The alcohol was getting weaker, though, and sleeping was harder each night. Would she have nightmares after this, or would she just forget?

The possibility scared her more than anything else. Every now and then the vivid memory of a life she took would boil up and overtake her, paralyzing her as she relived the murder. She would be sick with herself, wondering why she was allowed the temporary mercy of forgetting her life. Of forgetting her sin.

She wouldn't forget. She would try to remember these men, to remember Abigail and the duty that brought her down into the belly of the mine.

She stopped and reloaded her rifle, just in case. Then she reached to her right side and drew out her revolver. It'd be just as loud as the rifle, but the walls were getting narrower, aiming would be less difficult. Six bullets. If she was lucky, that's all she would need.

She could still see in the dark, one of the many "gifts" that her gods gave her. They "didn't want her missing a minute of it," they had explained to her as she wept. She was not proud of what she did on that day, how she had thrown herself at their mercy and begged for a death and an end. But her begging had only fueled their sadism. A never-ending life, never-dimming sight, and an increasingly high tolerance that would not even allow a reprieve in drunkenness.

Pan hated her gods. Hated them for controlling her life, for making her kill even now.

But, she had to admit, they made her good at it. Better than any Achilles had ever been.

A draft rushed with a form that slammed against her. In surprise, she dropped her revolver, screaming as a hand forced her face into the rough wall, cutting her skin and sending a trickle of tangy, copper blood to her tongue. She bit down her anger and surprise. An opponent even only a little bigger than her would have an advantage, and the man who pinned her was well over twice her size.

As his teeth reached for her throat, she brought her foot between his legs.

The man roared in anger and pain. Though the pestilence had overtaken him, his body was still a man's, with all the weaknesses that came with it.

She lifted his neck gently, exposing it so her knife's incision was neat and long. The black gore poured out of him, and after a long minute his corpse was paling into the dark pool beneath him.

She was panting, stomach churning and back aching from the fight. Hand-to-hand was not her specialty, though she had been taught by a few masters in Africa and East Asia. She found it too messy, too uncertain and unreliable. Uncomfortable and intimate, she preferred her opponents to keep their distance whenever she could help it.

She leaned against the wall of the mine and breathed slowly, quieting the roaring drum in her head. She lifted her hands, watching them shake in electric panic.

*Breathe.*

She could hear the furious wind far away, the flurries of snow and frost that had kept all this sickness buried for centuries. The wind blew through the tunnels, coming from behind her and boring down into the caverns below. There was no response, no shuffling of feet, and no unthinking, reflexive grunts. Even though she knew it was too naïve, too hopeful, she allowed herself to believe that she was alone.

She smiled, bowing her head into her gore-crusted hands.

The black ichor was too thin, too scentless to have come from anything living. Or maybe the air was too cold for the rot to stink. Whatever it was, she was glad for the small mercy.

She lifted herself up and away from the wall.

She picked up her revolver and moved forward alone, with no sounds other than those of her boots grinding against the dirt with staggering, uneven steps. She hummed to herself an old song in a language no longer spoken. The walk lasted miles. The men must have been desperate to have dug so deep.

They should have known better.

Then she came to it, the spot where the mines ended and the tunnels began. Pan wondered what they thought they found when they discovered this patch of hollow earth, when their picks struck a stone wall only to crack through to open spaces. A ruined mine wall hung open, stones haphazardly moved to the side so walking through was easier.

The walls of the tunnels were smooth, made by natural erosion and the burrowing of some gigantic worm. What made them had probably been there for thousands of years, biding its time before breaking the surface.

She wondered how many troubles were writhing down there, and if she would have to hunt them down more often as mankind continued to assert its ambition over a world it had no chance of controlling. Immortality would be even more exhausting if that was the case.

Her boot slipped beneath her, sending her sliding down the tunnels. Her hands shot out, but only found cool, smooth tunnel wall.

"Shit! Shit!"

She spread her arms and legs, hoping to slow herself as wind roared in her ears. The water clung to her coat, but there were no stones to catch. Finally, her hand hit a groove in the tunnel floor and she grabbed it at once, jerking her shoulder as it snapped back the weight of her body.

She hissed, pausing for a moment before she stood.

She was only a few feet away from an edge, though she couldn't see how steep the drop was. Carefully, she lifted herself and took a single step forward.

She would have fallen about forty feet.

The ground below was covered in loose pebbles and black mud, washing against the shores of an underground lake. The surface was flat and still. She picked up a stone at her feet and tossed it into the lake. It entered the water with a gentle *plop* that echoed for minutes in the yawning cavern.

The surface of the water began to move, boiling and writhing in fury.

"Right, then."

A long, sharp head emerged, glowing and bulbous blind eyes lined against pale, scaled skin. Its long, serpentine body was as dark as the cavern around it, giving its head the appearance of a floating cow skull. The spikes across its back were jagged and uneven, and at the end of its long, narrow mouth it hissed to reveal rows of narrow angler-fish teeth.

Black gore leaked from between them as it turned towards her. Its bulbous eyes widened.

It wasn't blind at all.

Before she had time to shout, the trouble rammed its head into the cavern wall beneath her, sending her wobbling as she slipped to meet the ground forty feet below.

## IV

Through the dim hum of her head, voices were laughing at her. Beautiful wind chime laughter, playful and innocent, laced with the venom of a sardonic and cruel joke. Loud, bellowing laughter of deep lungs and immeasurable power. She was running, pleading, screaming and crying across an unseen and never-ending canvas.

"*You're even better than I expected,*" a sonorous, velvet male voice purred.

She bolted up in the mud and grime, panting furiously as she realized the voice was a memory.

Only a memory.

The trouble towered above her, leering as her bones snapped back together and her bleeding flesh sealed itself shut. Its white wide eyes watched curiously, in reverence and awe as Pan put herself back together. She winced and cried, electric fires spewing from her joints and the small vertebrae across her neck. Hot tears welled up, uncontrollable and unstoppable as they broke the dam of her screaming.

It'd be easier to die, she thought, than put herself back together.

"Awww..." the trouble proclaimed above her. Its voice was high-pitched and grating, the voice of a sore-throated child.

"So that is what this is."

She picked herself up and moved her arms, making sure that her body still worked. She looked up, standing straight as possible to consider the trouble.

Pan had never encountered one that could speak before.

Maybe she could reason with it.

"I was a small thing when I first escaped."

She let it speak, feeling her neck to make sure the real weapon was still where she left it. But her neck was bare. The thin chain of her necklace must have snapped in the fall. She'd need to stall the trouble so she could look for it, otherwise she wouldn't stand a chance. She began pacing, pretending to listen intently to the trouble as she scanned the ground for a small, ornate wooden box.

"Set loose into a wide, open night. My brothers and sisters...gods...we were *legion*, writhing into the open air to set loose our divine duty upon mankind. I buried myself deep, waiting to gain strength and power. I knew I'd be found eventually; mankind is self-destructive, after all. I only wished to aid them in the endeavor."

It laughed, and Pan shuddered.

"Of all the things I expected to see when I was finally unearthed, I never expected it would be you, *Mother*."

She stopped looking for the box and froze. The word was accusatory, a lash against her very soul. She turned to the serpent defiantly, pointing a finger to its too-pleased-with-itself skeleton smile.

"Don't call me that."

It laughed again, shaking the roof of the cavern above it.

"What would I call you, then? You were the one that set us loose on the world, the one who sent us forward as emissaries of divine will." It lowered its head to her level, closer to examine and mock her. "You unleashed us to do good."

She shook her head, scanning the ground as she talked.

"There's nothing good about what you do."

It paused and twisted its head to the side, questioning and inquisitive.

"Is mankind not too aspirational for its own good? Do they not damage their only and sacred world? Are they not vainglorious and cruel?"

"No more than their gods," Pan spat.

She still could see them when she closed her eyes. They were beautiful beyond words, which only made their cruelty more pronounced and evil. They had adorned her with gifts, showered her with love and praise. Lovely, kind Aphrodite. Apollo, moving in the graceful, dancing way of a warrior-poet. And Zeus, whose smile glistened like dew and flared like lightning.

And then they gave her the jar.

"You speak blasphemy." It seemed frightened and indignant, an innocent being challenged and shaken.

"No, just telling you how I feel. Maybe you can sympathize. What is it that you do to people? Spread sickness? How is that a good thing?"

"It's what they *deserve*," the trouble hissed.

"We shouldn't get what we deserve," Pan responded. Her eyes fell on the box, no bigger than a pen case, lodged between two pebbles. The thin chain which had kept it around her neck had been broken in the fall, strung out in flayed angles around the box. But it was still intact, the painted wooden surface covered with oils that made it nearly indestructible.

"Justice is never pretty," she added, moving towards her weapon as she kept her eyes on the monster.

The trouble watched her slowly, its eyes shining in the dark like portals to Hades. It hummed, seeming to consider her words. Pan thought of how long the trouble had been in the dark and began to pity it. No doubt it had grown mad, angry. If it was anything like her, it hated itself.

"And the ones who deserve justice rarely get it anyway," she added softly.

The monster shook its head.

"You're *lying*. The gods created me for a reason. Just as they created *you* for a reason."

She shook her head, only a few steps away from the box. If she didn't get it, she'd be down here forever. The trouble could spend eternity tearing her apart, just like poor Prometheus.

"They didn't have a fucking *reason* for making me. They were just *sadistic* and *bored*."

"NO!" it roared, rearing up its neck and arching it for a strike. "They made you what you are so that you could *suffer*. Because you *deserve* it!"

It lunged at her, its jaws open to expose all its long, needle-teeth. She fell to her knee and drew her revolver, firing two shots into its left eye. They eye burst like a rotten orange, spilling luminous white blood into the water below. Her hands came down on the box, and without taking a moment for pause, she opened it.

First there was nothing.

Then a small rectangle of light.

The rectangle grew brighter and larger as the cavern burst into a blazing fire. The walls shook, setting stones and stalactites crashing down. The trouble screamed in terror and pain. A stone cracked against its back and it fell, its mouth falling open as it cried out.

"You monster!" it roared out.

"Get in the box, you spooky shit!" she roared back.

It wept, the suffocating, stifling crying of a horrified child that could not understand its suffering. Its form collapsed, fading away as it folded in on itself. As the light consumed it, the trouble became a shadow, growing narrower and narrower until it was little more than a long, dark worm.

Little more than a black, writhing thread.

There was a final, weak whisper.

"You *deserve* it."

She snapped the box lid closed. The cave around her was quiet now, and above her the mineshaft loomed high.

"She deserved it," it had said.

She gritted her teeth and placed the box in a coat pocket, throwing herself at the stone wall and gripping her hand against a jutting stone.

V

Abigail did not respond when Pan finished her story.

Outside, the trolleys moved slowly, their mechanical creaks rising into the air to match the cawing of the seagulls above. Pan's hand was itching for her flask, and she strummed her hands nervously waiting for Abigail's response.

"They're *all* dead?" Abigail finally ventured, allowing a little hope to penetrate her voice.

But Pan nodded.

"They all died when the monster died. It grabbed onto them, made their lives its own. They couldn't survive without it."

She wouldn't tell Abigail how many of the men she killed herself. There was no need to get into the gruesome details.

"What should I do now?" Abigail asked.

Pan laughed, perhaps a bit colder than she needed to be.

"Go back, go forward, it doesn't matter. Just put all this behind you. You're young, you've got a whole life to live."

Abigail nodded, mustering a weak smile.

"Thank you, for whatever you did out there..."

She slid an envelope across Pan's desk. Pan contemplated not taking it, feeling some level of revulsion from taking a bunch of money from a newly minted widow. But she needed to pay bills, and any money would do.

Pan slid the envelope into her shirt pocket.

"Nothing to it. Just try your best to be happy, Abigail. It's important."

The young girl nodded. "Well, thank you anyway."

Abigail's flowery dress left and closed the door behind it.

Alone at last, Pan drew her flask from her desk. Its grey surface showed her reflection. A pretty face with sad, deep eyes. Tired eyes.

Considering those eyes, the flask felt heavier in her hands.

She wondered if she could put it away, leave it back to its prison desk drawer. She could go for a walk and take her own advice, maybe watch the sunset and flirt with some kind man who could help her forget her problems for just one night. One good night in a long, long life.

She could take her own advice and live her life, put all her troubles behind her.

But then the reflection in the glass changed. Instead of a beautiful young woman, a bearded man looked back at her, white eyes and black gore bleeding from between his lips. A corpse-white man, choking as his neck was collapsed by her strong hands. The illusion faded, and her own face returned.

Still beautiful. Still unscarred.

She didn't bother with a glass.

**Author's Notes:** It's difficult to ignore the misogyny of western creation myths. Eve luring Adam. Pandora. I don't know where I first read that in the original myth, Pandora herself was the punishment of the gods to mankind for accepting Prometheus' gift of fire. But the idea stuck with me. From there it went to a new version of Pandora, someone who didn't die but who struggled with survivor's guilt nonetheless. A swashbuckling gunslinger, a pirate, a timeless adventurer.

In truth, Pandora figures pretty largely in a set of shared universe stories I work on every now and then concerning a family of occult detectives and spies called "The Bartreds." She hasn't yet revealed herself to young Joe Bartred, and characteristic of an immortal with revenge and heroism on the mind, has a long plan to make things right.

# I Keep It in a Little Box

I

IT WAS HELL. It *had* to be.

Tom had never been in a darker, lonelier place. And, all things considered, there were really only *two* places he thought he *could* be.

His hands slid across sharp, cold gravel. His knees and palms were burning, caked in stinging cuts and cooling blood. He shifted uncomfortably, bringing the back of his hand to his forehead to wipe away unknown grime and sweat. He breathed slowly, taking cold and soothing breaths into his lungs and holding them.

The pounding of his head dimmed and he strained his ears. A breath of wind crossed an unseen body of water as he heard the gentle slopping of small waves against a calm surface. Tom remembered that, according to Dante's *Inferno*, there were rivers in Hell. He shuddered, remembering the other things *Inferno* described.

The other things that might be waiting for him.

But if this was Hell, where was his torment?

Was it Hell to simply be alone with his thoughts in the dark?

The idea shook him. His entire life he had tried to escape his own thoughts; his entire life, they had been more devastating than any weapon or any word. Nothing terrified him more than the eyes that lurked in his mirror or the cold, stagnant voice that reassured him that he was not worth anything.

Not worth anything at all.

And to be alone with that voice...

It would be a familiar Hell.

He stepped forward and squinted. It was useless; the world was no different when his eyes were open than when they were shut. He took another step and felt a familiar weight in his pocket. Cautiously, he removed his phone.

No signal, of course, and the time display was gone.

There probably wasn't a charger anywhere nearby, so he'd need to be careful.

He turned the phone away from him and let its screen illuminate what little it could. In one direction there was nothing, the light only extending two feet before it was swallowed into the emptiness. In another, the phone's light glistened off a wavering surface. He slid its screen to darkness and walked in the direction of the water.

Through the darkness he felt a cold, damp breeze. Wind was coming from across the lake, and if there was wind, there might be a way out. His feet slipped on the rocks, and he flailed his arms to keep himself up and tightened his grip on his phone. Tom regained his balance, breathing heavily as he swiped the phone's screen and once again used it for light.

He could not see the end of the lake, which seemed vaster and wider than any ocean. White, bulbous fish with sleek skin broke the water. Realizing he was thirsty, he reached down and cupped his hands to take a long drink. The water was cold and metallic, dirt pooling at the bottom of his hands. He spat out bitter mud and peered out again.

A large, pale catfish leapt, thrashing and barking as it fed on a low-flying moth. He supposed that there would be enough there to survive on, assuming he could learn to catch the catfish. He knew people used to eat raw meat, and imagined that though he may be sick at his first meal, his stomach and immune system would adjust.

The shore he was standing on was covered in rocks and shale, sharp things that should have broken bones rather than merely scraped. Maybe some of these stones were flint. Maybe he could make a fire.

He could walk along the shore of the lake, to see if there was a way to the other side.

To see *if* there was another side.

There would be nothing but time in this place.

Above the surface of the lake, a blue light broke.

The light was little more than a dot, shifting between dark indigo and bright, neon azure. It seemed to waver and lurch with unseen breath, moving slowly and steadily. The light was too far away for Tom to clearly see its source, though it appeared to be some sort of tower lined with small, round stones.

Then the tower moved.

There was the whoosh of wings that cut the air, the hiss of claws that scraped the water. A catfish barked as it was seized. A flame shot out to kill and cook it at once. In that moment, Tom saw the thing that was flying towards him.

He ran.

But his legs were hurt, his body slow, his mind reeling. He didn't get far before a wall of blue fire shot up before him. He stopped, sliding uncontrollably towards the flames before a cold, clawed hand grabbed him gently and stopped him.

He trembled as the claws met across his chest, crying as they let him go.

"Little thing."

The voice was deep and booming, filling the darkness completely. It was soothing yet scraping, each word followed by long pauses and reptile hisses.

"Little thing...you are safe."

Tom turned, blinking through tears. In the light of the flames, he could see the dragon in all its terrifying detail.

The thing perched on its four legs like a dog sitting upright, leathery wings folded at its side. It had no soft underbelly, but was covered in armored, obsidian scales that gleamed and glistened like water. Its neck was long and winding, curving down like a snake so its blind, milky eyes could meet his own on his level. Its head was pointed and sharp, crowned with two horns that curled like a proud and regal ram.

It spoke again, fully revealing sharp teeth and a long, pallid tongue.

Its breath stank of methane and raw fish with each slow word.

"What is...your name, little thing?"

"T-Tom."

"Tom...how did you come to be here?"

Panic rose as Tom recalled his final moments before he woke up on the shore of the dark lake.

"Am I dead?" Tom asked, his voice cracking with fear.

The dragon snorted, a jet of fire escaping its nose in irritation. "And how would you...expect me to know a thing like that?"

Tom was silent, dumbfounded.

"*Tom...*" it hissed. "How did you come to be here?"

Tom confessed, the words falling out of him without control, "I don't know. I just jumped off the cliff and woke up here. I promise. I'm sorry. Please don't hurt me!"

Despite everything else he hated about himself, Tom was never a coward. He had gotten into his share of ill-planned and one-sided fights, taken his bruises and left them too. But there was no way he was going to fight a dragon, no way he could even begin to *try*.

The dragon hummed, thinking. Somewhere a fish leapt.

"Are you...a fairy?"

"What?" Tom responded.

"Do you...have wings?"

"No, of course not."

"Then why?" The dragon craned its long neck down. Its face came to level with Tom's, its milky eyes peering directly into his soul. "Why would you do such a thing...if you cannot fly?"

Tom gulped.

"I-I wanted to die."

## II

"Grab a beer and put on a brave face."

That was all Katy had wanted him to do. For any normal person, it would have been easy. She was coming from a good place, from the kindest heart. She *understood* him, and her desire to make him happy and whole was always well-intended. Sometimes she was successful. No one could make him smile like her, whether it was stroking his ear as they kissed or singing a song as she walked down the hall.

"Grab a beer and put on a brave face."

It had been something he used to say to himself, back when he was still in college and he was expected to go to parties. He was good looking enough, but he always felt alone in loud, crowded places. Where everyone else was having a good time, losing themselves to rhythms and each other, Tom would drown in his own thoughts. It was a contradiction he hated about himself, that he always made people so sad when they were so happy.

Katy had caught him saying this mantra to himself in the mirror once, and from that point on she used the phrase carefully, to remind him that he was stronger than he thought.

She was far too good for him, and he knew that. She must have known it too, deep down somewhere. He'd told her before, but it only made her angry when he said that there was somebody out there who was better for her.

Someone with a kinder heart. Someone who was less work. Someone she wouldn't pity.

The loss of his parents, his dad only dying a year after his mom, had taken down the pillars of his life. He hadn't realized how much talking to them meant, how idle chats about food and heated arguments about politics had kept him going. They were divorced, but they had always done right by him. Mom went peacefully, unexpectedly in her sleep. Dad had an unexpected stroke in his workshop while everyone had been away.

That was what kept Tom awake, what made him cry every morning since. The thought of his father alone on the floor, unable to move. Had he been panicking while he died? Had he been praying? Had he been thinking of Tom? He imagined the hunger, the fear and the misery, and hated himself for not being there to hold his father as he left the world.

Katy seemed to understand. It was the sort of thing that would have caused *anyone* to break down. But for Tom, who felt things so profoundly and differently, the loss was catastrophic. His appetite vanished, he would avoid sleeping as long as possible and then dread waking up when he did. Outside the confines of the apartment, the world became too loud, too sprawling, and too hostile. The idea of venturing beyond it was a weight on his back, a paralyzing thought that made him physically sick. He preferred being alone more than ever.

He went through the motions of his job, but refused to do more than that. He would leave home as late he could and return as soon as he could. He would talk to his little sister when he could, until she began to get too close to uncovering how truly unwell he was. Then he would end their conversations briefly, making pretexts to escape the phone.

Katy respected his need to grieve, and gave him his space and time. But he was beginning to not take care of himself. The lack of sleep and proper diet was ruining his mind, his skin, and his already poisonous mood. Tom knew that if he did not do something soon, he could do real, long-term damage to himself.

Then, Katy attempted to offer him a way out. He took it, more for her than himself, agreeing to venture outside for a "small get-together" at a friend's house. But the house had been sprawled with people, warm bodies whose loud noises and wild movements forced him towards a wall. There had been a live band, a keg of crisp, flavorless beer. Red plastic cups.

He had been uncomfortable, and so he stepped outside for just a moment.

On his way out, he saw Katy. Smiling, dancing with her girlfriends, for all of the world looking as if she was unburdening herself. Her smile wide, her long, curly blonde hair swaying with her hips. The happiest she had been in weeks.

That's when he decided.

···

Tom hadn't told Katy about his plan. He left her a note, though he wasn't sure that it would help. She may be sad at first, but years later she would come to admit that he had been a drag on her. He would keep her back, he would keep hurting her, and that was not something he could live with.

So he wouldn't.

When she went to see her parents, he smiled and said he would be okay by himself for the weekend. He took time in writing the note, making sure that he explained himself as tenderly and gently as he could. He crumpled three drafts before he finally wrote something he was okay with. Then, he went out and bought the most expensive bourbon he could afford, the sort of thing he had always wanted to buy for a special occasion.

When night came, he took his car up the twisting roads to the mountains just outside of Taos. He carefully drove through the winding roads, smiling as the black bears rummaged through roadside trashcans and gave him scared, innocent looks in his car headlights. He got to a spot not far from a cliff that he had daydreamed about a few times before.

He pulled over.

He sat there, drinking his bottle of bourbon and sighing as the burn lovingly slid down his throat and warmed his stomach. The stars were bright, like someone had cracked open the sky to let them spread far and wide across a black canvas. The air was cold, the wind carrying a chill gently through the tall pines. Somewhere an owl hooted and night birds sang.

He thought of the people he would miss. His brother, on some boat off the shores of Nicaragua with the coast guard. His little sister, still probably worried about him. He left her a note, too, explaining that she needed to be good and remember not to blame herself.

And Katy.

Poor Katy.

Tom finished his bourbon. He decided to do it before he talked himself out of it.

He was already drunk, so it would be easy.

He sighed, slipping an arm over his mouth and running forward.

The air cut along him, wind rising up to deafen his pounding heart.

The world went dark.

### III

Tom finished his story, surprised to find his eyes dry and voice even.

The dragon seemed to consider the story, lifting its head up towards the darkness and growling. For long minutes, spits of blue flame sparked and died in its clenched teeth, giving Tom only brief moments of sight in the all-consuming darkness.

"I know...this feeling," the dragon finally spoke, as if to answer the entirety of Tom's story with one sentence.

"Loneliness," the dragon spoke again. "Isolation. These are...horrible weights. I am...*tired* myself. Tell me of the world...how does it fair?"

"Wh-what do you mean?"

"Are there...still *wars*?"

"Yes, of course," Tom added.

"Do humans...exacerbate their own circumstances...as they have done before? Do they...ruin their earth? Do they starve...each other?"

"Yes, still. Maybe now more than ever." Tom sighed, and the dragon sighed too.

"And you...sought to end it? Your...suffering?"

"Yes."

The dragon nodded, understanding.

"Would you...like to end it? *All* suffering?"

"What do you mean?"

The dragon spread its massive wings, knocking Tom down when it lifted itself off the ground. Tom coughed, the sour contents of his upset stomach jolted by yet another fall. He blinked, watching the dragon's blue flame as it crossed the lake once more, settling in some far away spot as a distant, dying star. Then it returned, landing about thirty feet away from Tom, deeper into the darkness. A claw came up and bent inward, and Tom approached the dragon cautiously.

Before the dragon was a simple wooden box, small with a rusted, iron latch.

Tom reached for it, but the dragon stopped him, swiping at him with its tail.

"I keep it there...just as I have always kept it."

"Kept what?"

The dragon lowered his face once more to Tom's, its hazy, useless eyes only inches from his own.

"The end of the world."

## IV

It had not always been the *only* dragon.

There had been others. Never *many*, but others.

They had taken pity on mankind, starving things afraid of the dark and vulnerable to the cold. The dragons had descended among the men, bringing them fire. And with the fire mankind sharpened stones, melted metals, and told stories more dangerous than any weapon.

They forgot what the dragons once did for them and created untruths from distant recollections and vague impressions. The dragons had always been the guardians of the world's end, though they no longer remembered how they ever received such a duty, let alone from what authority.

Mankind came to fear dragons, to fear their life-giving fire, their looming shadows and mystifying words. The dragons were recast as greedy, cruel things. Soon, the box which contained the end of the world became the most coveted and misunderstood object of mankind's hateful legends.

And the hunt began.

The work of ruthless centuries, of determined and delusional executioners. Reluctantly, the dragons would slay them, grotesquely decorating the entrances of their lairs with the remains of warriors to deter men from their foolishness. But the follies of mankind proved to be many and bloody. More warriors came, with better armor and sharper swords. They came in waves, unconcerned with the lives of comrades who fell beside them, willing to sacrifice ten of themselves for the death of one dragon.

And while the dragons were few, mankind was many.

The remaining dragons sought isolation, never keeping the box in the same location for more than a few decades at a time. But even in the tallest mountains and the darkest swamps, their persecutors were determined and ever-willing.

A hundred became a dozen. A dozen became five. Five became one.

So, it hid. It hid in a deeper, darker place than any of its kind had ever gone before. It contented itself to survive only on generations of blind fish, to lose its eyes to millennia of sightlessness. It began to dwell less on its loneliness and more on the maintenance of its body, becoming as much an animal as the fish it consumed. Hunger and exhaustion became the only things it tended to and, in time, it forgot the world.

## V

The dragon's story made Tom ashamed, the sort of sad fairytale an exile would sing about their burned homeland and a childhood that they could never return to. A nostalgia for better and worse times alike.

"How old *are* you?" Tom ventured.

The dragon snorted, angrily dismissing the question.

"You...measure time...*arbitrarily*. Your units of measurement would...be insufficient in...measuring my age."

"But how are you not dead?" Tom asked. "Wouldn't you have died a long time ago? All of this darkness, this loneliness, only eating one thing, it can't be good for you."

"Dragons do not die...of natural causes."

Tom considered this.

The dragon pointed a claw towards the unassuming wooden box.

"What do you...then propose?"

"If I opened it," Tom asked, "how would the world end?"

There was a short gasping sound, perhaps a laugh.

"I do not know...it has never been opened."

"Ah."

Tom paused, narrowing his eyes at the box. It was about the size of a shoebox, unassuming and worn with time. He lifted it up, shaking it to see if something inside would scream or curse.

Nothing.

It felt empty, though the wood was thick and heavy.

He pressed his ear against it.

Again, nothing.

He looked at it for a long time, studying the simple latch which kept it shut. He thought of his mother and father, smiling and gone forever. He thought of his own misery and misery he would never know. He thought of the desperation of war orphans in collapsing houses, the crushing sadness of a starving mother giving up her own food so that her thinning child might eat. He thought of the greed which compelled the actions of nations, the lust which made machines that ground people into blood and dust.

Perhaps the universe would be cosmically better without the world. Maybe the universe did not need a human stain to spill over and ruin all the beautiful places it had never been and was never meant to go to.

Then his mind wandered to Katy. Her hair brushing against him in the morning. Her funny smile, her rolling eyes after he told a stupid joke. He thought of that smile, of all the things it meant. Of all the things it could do.

He thought of that smile, and thought of what it had to say:

"Put on a brave face."

"What...does this mean?" the dragon asked, a genuine tone of confusion rising from the depths of its throat.

"It means..." Tom held out the box, placing it back into the dragon's opening palm. "That I don't think I should open the box."

The dragon did not reach back for the box. It regarded Tom coldly, its breath subsided into a slow growl. Tom pulled the box back towards his chest, taking a few steps away.

Though its eyes were milky, Tom could see anger welling in the dragon's fanged scowl. It lowered its head to the level of Tom's chest, moving lithely and quietly as a crouching panther. The tension welled up from the shadows, and every nerve became alive and electric as Tom began to understand that the thing was going to pounce on him.

"You...said that mankind still...bleeds against itself..."

"Y-yes?" Tom balked, walking back further as the dragon approached.

"You are still...lonely...and sad...despite everything?"

"Well–"

"Do you not...believe that there are *others* like you...whose suffering you could end? Do you not believe...that there are those who have earned...oblivion? An escape from...this darkness?"

Tom slipped on some gravel beneath him. A rock cut into his palm, and he bit his lip to stop himself from screaming.

"Do you not...believe...that the good deserve their rest...and the wicked deserve their end?"

"I don't understand." Tom found his courage. "If you think the box needs to be opened, if you think you need to get out of this place so badly, why not just open it?"

The dragon stopped, caught off guard. It sat still for a moment.

"I...cannot."

Tom pressured forward, catching the dragon's reluctance.

"Why not? You don't need thumbs to open it. You've had all this time."

The dragon bared its teeth, long white things that glistened as blue fire welled up behind its throat.

"Open the box," the dragon commanded coldly.

"No."

The dragon opened its mouth wide.

Tom turned and ran. The jets of flames came fast, and he bobbed and weaved in zigzags to avoid them as they shot out. Behind him the dragon's feet pounded as it roared in frustration. Tom's lip bled from biting down, the only way he could keep himself from screaming. He knew he was lucky that the dragon was blind. That this would be over quickly if he made more noise than was absolutely necessary.

"Stop running...little thing!" the dragon roared.

But he would not stop running. He ran faster and more frantically than he ever had in his life. He did not know if there was a place he could hide, or a way he could get out.

But he had to try.

"You are...not brave enough...to end your suffering...to end your being. So I will do it...*for* you!"

But it wasn't fear moving him forward. At least, not fear of dying. There was something else, something that bubbled from his subconscious mind to almost make itself heard above the clamoring from his chest.

"One moment of pain...and it will all be done...just stop running."

But he *couldn't* stop. He could only think of his little sister. His brother. Katy. He had never meant to hurt them, not once in his life. He wouldn't let their world end.

Fire caught his shoes. He screamed out as his soles melted beneath him, sending him reeling forward.

The box flew from his hands.

The dragon stopped. Tom stopped. For horrible seconds, the world was quiet.

*Click.*

The dragon ceased breathing, quieting its flapping wings. The fish did not jump, the water did not move. Tom looked on, horrified and compelled.

The box rested, open and empty.

And then, a small rectangle of brilliant white light emerged from the depths of the box. Around them the darkness fell away like drying paint chips. Beneath him the ground shook, trembling as the world roared. The darkness fell away faster, and the spots of light, once so many stars, began to merge into a blinding, soothing white screen. Tom could finally see himself. He could see how cut, how broken he was.

But he could see.

He turned to the dragon in terror. It was fading away, its form falling off to merge with the sterile, shining nothingness. Its eyes were black now, its throat emitting something of a loud, pleasant chuckle.

"Goodness...an end to this world. An end to...this suffering."

The dragon fell away, piece by piece, until only its knowing eyes remained, shedding slow tears.

Then those too were gone, and Tom was hurtling through the white void, screaming and thrashing.

## VI

He was striking at the air. The sun hung directly above him, blinding him and worsening a roaring, throbbing headache. His skin was red and tight with sunburns. His stomach shook, nausea overtaking him quickly.

He bolted up, desperately trying to see where he was. The white-grey cliff-face towered before him, the green of the tall pines taunting him playfully from their high perches along its side.

He reached into his pocket but felt the cracked, sliding fragments of his broken phone. No help, then.

Not this time.

He didn't know how he was going to get back up. He knew it was going to be hard, that every moment would be a struggle.

But his survival depended on it.

And, despite himself, he was smiling.

*For Christopher Ropes.*
*Despite ourselves, we're smiling.*

**Author's Notes:** "I Keep It in a Little Box" is a deeply personal story, an old idea which I'd struggled for years to put into words. For three summers I worked on a ranch in northern New Mexico, where the nearest "big town" was Taos. I like to describe myself as a "self-educated extrovert," and really learned how to have a big personality in this context. The setting, my emotions at the time, informed this story. About a young man in the darkest sorts of depression and an easy step away from dying.

The impetus of this story came from a call for a charity anthology dedicated to my friend, Christopher Ropes. Christopher remains one of our best writers in the field, and is himself someone who is quite open about his mental and emotional health. My friendship with him has made me more comfortable in my own mind when it's roaring, and in my own soul when it's sinking. This story is still for you, BRopes. Despite ourselves, we're smiling.

# The Death of an Author

SOMEHOW, JILLIAN WAS alone in the hospice center.

Everything had gone quiet around three o'clock in the morning, and now she sat behind the long, wooden console desk and wheeled her chair to peek into different patients' rooms. The hallway light was a soft comfort against the darkness of those open doors, where the machines monitoring vitals beeped and moaned as family members slept next to their departing loved ones. The air was cool, wafting memories of dark, summer lakeshore breezes. Jillian was fighting desperately to stay awake. Caffeine, her third espresso today, and random internet searches (Mark Twain's real name was "Samuel Clemens," and O. Henry was actually "William Sydney Porter") kept her exhaustion at bay.

Because of her kind smile and calm demeanor, she had come to learn every one of her patients' stories, but none had intrigued her so much as Arthur Ickes, who was departing this earth at 82 years old. In episodes of half-consciousness, he presented himself as a happy man who loved to laugh but, heartbreakingly, no longer had the energy for it. His hair had only thinned slightly as the treatment took everything else from him. He had a wide nose, perfect for resting thick, comical glasses on. He no longer wore his glasses. These days, his eyes were almost always closed. He was smallish, even more so as the meat was stripped away from him and he was reduced to a thin existence beneath his bedsheets.

But he was funny, called her pretty and poked fun at himself when he could.

"I suppose I'll want myself donated, when I'm done," he had told her.

"That's very brave of you, Arthur."

"Hell... I won't need any of it then."

His youngest son was the only one left who could visit him. Sam lived two hours away and somehow made it up every night.

Unfortunately, his father was often asleep by then. She had come to know Sam and his big family, his wife Maria and daughters Isabell and Lizzie. He carried photos of them in his wallet, and with each visit he left a new one next to his father's bed. Most of the time, though, he just held Arthur's hand, stroked his hair, and smiled.

Sam was young, too early in years and career to be able to escape for a full day with his father during the work week. He could bring up his kids for the weekend, but as Arthur worsened Sam apparently made the decision that his girls did not need to see their grandpa so sick. So, Sam's visits became routine and lonely ones.

But one day, he brought something which Jillian had never seen before.

Sam came in wearing a large hiking backpack. He slung it off his shoulders and took out three Walmart bags stuffed with magazines. He handed a stack to Jillian and she leafed through the faded covers, gleaming with plastic and watercolors. They had names like *Tales of Wonder* and *Astonishing Adventures*, pictures of eerily enchanting monsters and buxom women in various poses of distress. She gave them a confused, worried look.

"*Don't fault Dad for this. 'Sex sells,' right?*"

Before she could ask what this had to do with Arthur, he explained:

"*See that name?*" He pointed to the magazine she was holding, in thick-white print where it read, "Featuring: Ian Acroix."

"*That's Dad.*"

And so began Jillian's late-night search for information on pen names and Ian Acroix.

Looking across her computer screen, it seemed that Ian Acroix was quite the name in his field. He had begun in the late 50s, spilling out of the shadows of someone called H. P. Lovecraft and another named Clark Ashton Smith. She didn't know who either of them were, and couldn't understand half of the stories attributed to Ian Acroix. His stories had titles like "Fantasmagoria" and "The Shadow of Uchtritl," and as she read them, she often found herself lost in thick description without the guidance of anything resembling a plot.

What characters she could identify in the stories were more unrealistic than those she usually read about, when she read at all. Jillian had gotten bad about reading, as her life got more and more in the way. First school, then more school, with a marriage and two small children.

A divorce, as amicable as possible, and fights over scheduling and coordinating with the kids as they kept getting bigger. By the time she had any moments to herself, her mind and eyes were too heavy to give any attention to pages. Too often, she glued herself to some stupid (and wholly inaccurate) medical drama and fell asleep for one blissful hour before waking back up and slipping into bed beside her boyfriend.

When she did read, when she *could* read, it was Jodi Picoult or Tom Clancy, books she had picked up in airports before long flights that could be read by the pool and over the frosted rime of a margarita. Ian Acroix's style was less formulaic, one might even say *formula-less*. His characters included cursed warriors, vampires, necromancers, and space-faring aliens. Their settings were war-torn fantasy worlds of cursed forests and high castles, haunted post-apocalyptic landscapes and dying planets at the edge of an expanding cosmos.

It was too far off the beaten path to be her cup of tea.

But there had been a fanbase when Arthur was still writing. Ian Acroix was famous for actively writing back to his fans, encouraging generations of writers to continue their work after they faced rejections from editors, or succumbed to depression and the shadows of conceived inadequacy. But it seemed that the stories were never put together in collected volumes, despite pleas from fans, and consequently Acroix's readership dwindled. Going to his website, Jillian saw that no one had bothered to update it in the last five years.

Not since Arthur had first learned he was terminally ill.

A loud thud brought her eyes up from the computer screen.

A man now stood on the other side, his knuckles knocking politely on the wood to get her attention. He was at least six-and-a-half feet tall, clad ("clad," Jillian thought to herself) in black-grey armor. Skulls and leaves were etched into the pattern of the plates, with thin chain mail covering every other part of him but his face. It was a narrow, mirthless face framed by thick black hair almost long enough to conceal the hilt of the sword on his back.

She reached for her cellphone, ready to call the police.

"Good madam." He spoke in a harsh voice. "I am here to see an old friend of mine, and I was hoping that you might point the way to his quarters."

"Sir..." She collected herself. The man looked like he had just come from some sort of convention, and it was too true that dying often attracted strange company. He would not be the first eccentric to visit a hospice center, but his was certainly the first *sword* she had seen there.

"You *cannot* bring a weapon in here."

He raised one eyebrow and gave a puzzled look. His eyes lit up, as if an obvious misunderstanding had been made clear, and he laughed. His laugh was dry but genuine, the subdued happiness of a man more used to sadness than smiles.

"Forgive me, but a sword is no weapon until removed from its sheath. Only *then*"—he held up a finger to accentuate his instruction—"is a sword a weapon. But I am Loki Crane, and my sword cannot leave my person. It is a spiritual attachment sewn into my very soul by the goddess Katerina of the Mountain Wind. You will find, however, that it likewise cannot spill any blood save in the keeping of peace...my burden to right my many wrongs."

"Nonetheless, Mr.... Crane." She looked around, stunned that there were no other hospice nurses in the building.

"Please, madam, the winds have told me that my friend does not have long to live—"

"Excuse me—"

She had not noticed the young woman who was standing next to Loki Crane. Jillian had not heard the doors open, nor had she heard the young woman walk across the linoleum floor to her desk. She couldn't have been older than 22. Her red hair reached all the way to the small of her back, ornamented with various bat-shaped pins and flaked with blonde-gold throughout. A tight red dress clung to her body, as ornamentally and intricately flaked with gold-seeming designs as her hair. Her eyes were bright red, almost like headlights. She smiled and revealed two long fangs.

"I'm looking for Mr. Acroix, too. My name is Allister and I am a...*very* old friend."

Loki Crane gave a weak smile as he faced the young woman. "We never did meet, but I have heard much of you."

"Likewise, Mr. Crane."

"I have heard," Loki Crane continued in his gravelly, harsh voice, "that you were sometimes the villain, and sometimes the hero. Sometimes good, often bad."

Allister's red lips lifted around her sharp fangs. "I believe, Mr. Crane, you are describing the vast majority of *everyone*."

"Look," Jillian interrupted. "Who *are* you people? Did you come from the same convention or something?"

They both looked at her, confused.

"We just told you, I'm Allister and this is Loki Crane. We're here to see Mr. Acroix."

She understood. These were fans, crazy fans who'd somehow learned Arthur was dying.

"Look," Jillian began. "Only family–"

"Excuse me."

Jillian looked around, searching for the voice but finding no one. It had been distinctly loud, as if the owner had been standing right next to her. Allister put on a wry, playful smile. Loki Crane nodded knowingly and pointed a large, gloved hand towards Jillian's shoulder.

She turned and screamed.

There, floating about half an inch above her shoulder, was a tiny man. He was about the size of a hummingbird and was surrounded on all sides by a thin, glowing fog that made him look like a tiny ghost. He was moving too fast, flashing in and out of her line of sight so that she could not get a focused look at him. Jillian swatted her arms reflexively, and when she hit him she felt the damp moisture of a cloud.

She fell out of her chair, trembling as the little man floated above her face.

"I'm looking for Mr. Acroix, can you tell me where his room is?"

Her mind reeled.

"I'm afraid you've scared the poor woman." She heard Allister's voice. "I think she hasn't quite understood what's happening yet."

"Ah."

The little man floated away, and Jillian pulled herself up to her desk.

The newcomer hovered above Allister's shoulder.

"This is Arian Lightfoot," Allister explained. "He hasn't quite learned social graces. He's more for children, you understand?"

Jillian couldn't think. She was tired, angry that strange people could just barge into a hospice facility and demand to see someone. She was even *angrier* that there was now a tiny ghost who she could not explain away as a hallucination. She clung desperately to her frustration, letting it be an anchor against disbelief and impossibility.

"I don't understand who you people think you are, what you think you're doing, or *what*," she pointed to Arian Lightfoot, "that *thing* is.

Furthermore, why do you think it is okay to just barge in on Mr. Ickes in the middle of the night?" she asked between frantic stammers.

Allister hit a beautifully manicured hand to a pale palm as if she had just remembered the answer to a riddle. Startled by her movement, Arian Lightfoot flew away from Jillian's view.

"That must be it! Forgive us, we only know him by Acroix. But yes, perhaps on this occasion Ickes is more appropriate."

"Excuse me."

Jillian folded her face into her hands and groaned. "I'm losing my mind, aren't I?"

"Don't be so dramatic." Loki Crane's voice was iron and cold. "Just because you encounter the unusual doesn't mean you're going mad. Be *reasonable.*"

"I didn't realize you were capable of irony, Mr. Crane," Allister quipped.

"Capable of what?"

"I said, *'excuse me'!*" the fourth voice chimed.

Looking up, Jillian saw a sickly man in a plaid shirt. His eyes were pointed, slanted like a cat's. His hair was mussed, his skin pulled tight and pale. Thin, greasy stubble splashed across his face. He would have seemed somewhat normal, if not for the fact that his hands were long, multi-jointed, and clawed.

"I'm looking for Mr.-"

"Ickes.," Allister interrupted.

"Who is that?"

"It's what they know Ian as in this place."

"I didn't think I would see you here," Loki Crane said.

"Of course," the man responded incredulously. He shook his head in disbelief before continuing: "I might not be the most"—he stopped to consider his next words—"praiseworthy individual, but I owe him just as much as *any of you.* I love him as much as *any of you.*"

Jillian groaned. "What exactly is your relationship to Mr. Ickes?"

"Woman, don't you get it by now?" the man in plaid roared.

"Be respectful," Loki Crane added grimly. "I cannot draw my sword, but there are no such restrictions on my fists."

The clawed man laughed, clutching his sides sarcastically. "We know how *that* would end, Loki Crane."

"Please," Jillian whimpered now. "You're going to wake up the other patients."

"I swear," Allister continued past Jillian's pleas. "Every time men meet there is this ritual of chest-beating. It's ridiculous, really. Would you calm down, both of you? King, will you let it rest?"

The clawed man, presumably King, looked at her for a moment.

"Unless," Allister continued, "you'd like to try your fight with *me*."

He seemed to think about it a moment and shook his head.

"No...I don't suppose I would. I've grown far too fond of you, and this occasion is too solemn for me to ruin it with your death."

Allister smiled with unveiled annoyance at King, then turned to Jillian. "We apologize. We're out of place here, and we are not entirely familiar with the customs. Please, could you tell us where the room is?"

"I am so sorry, but only family are allowed to visit," Jillian responded, firmly but with enough sadness to convey an attempt at sympathy.

"That's perfect," Allister said. "We're all his family."

"Oh." Jillian was caught. "How are you related?"

"I suppose you'd say we're all his children."

Before Jillian could argue, Arian Lightfoot was back.

"I've found it! I've found Ian's room."

"Thank you, Mr. Lightfoot." Loki Crane smiled, somehow grimly.

"Follow me," Lightfoot chimed back.

"Please don't?" Jillian asked one last time.

But the four of them were off, evoking a scene from *Wizard of Oz*. The hospice center, dimly lit, allowed their forms to slide in and out of sleepy darkness, their silent steps too inconspicuous to wake the sleeping residents and their families. Loki Crane's armor glinted with Allister's long hair. Jillian could no longer make out Arian Lightfoot by the time they reached the unlit portal of Arthur Ickes' room. The each walked in, one by one. King, the clawed man, stood at the door for a moment. Hesitant to enter, muttering to himself. Finally, he walked in.

Jillian was frozen, unsure of what was happening or what to do.

Finally, she got up and followed them into the room.

She covered her mouth to stifle her screams.

Arthur Ickes and his son were fast asleep. Arthur's chest was rising and falling, erratic and weak. Sam Ickes was slumped in an uncomfortable chair, book folded on his lap and neck tilting over the back of his chair. All around them were people and monsters of incredible size and variance. Loki Crane knelt at the foot of the bed with the reverence of a knight before their sovereign. Allister lovingly stroked Arthur's head, bent down and kissed him to leave a stain of wet, red lips on his forehead. Arian Lightfoot floated in the corner of the room, crying between the verses of a light, fluttering song.

A dragon overcrowded the room, coiling upon itself in a corner to take as little space as it could. Its purple, green, and golden body shone softly in the white light of the room, while its eyes glowed a bright emerald green and its mouth hung open slightly enough to let a floral smoke escape. It seemed that without moving its mouth, the beast was singing. And though she could not understand the words, Jillian was moved to tears by the low, humming rhythm that came from its deep, scaled throat.

Another figure, a tall, bearded man with a long black robe, sang along with the dragon's tune. With one hand he held a massive, worn book. With the other, he caressed the dragon's head, stroking it as if he were comforting a small and distraught young child. His eyes moved across the pages of his book, and as his song concluded he took a moment to clear his throat before he turned the page. Then, he and the dragon began a new song.

King stood at the side, along with other characters who looked uncomfortable in their company. Some of those who stood with him were horrible-looking monsters with burnt faces and twisted features, carrying axes and whips; others were plain looking, but had a darkness in their eyes that forced a long shiver out of Jillian.

"Where do you think he'll go?" King asked no one in particular.

Allister sighed. "Somewhere new, I hope."

"Indeed." Loki Crane rose from his kneel. "I cannot imagine him ever resting, certainly not *eternally*. No...he'll go on to a new adventure, I imagine."

"A whole other world," King added.

"Yes...yes, I suppose that is one way to think about it," a voice Jillian could not identify spoke.

"It's what he'd want," a man in some sort of streamlined, white spacesuit added.

"Maybe he'll get to come with us?" Arian Lightfoot suggested meekly.

Loki Crane laughed wistfully. "Yes, that'd be something, I suppose."

One by one, the guests moved and shifted their position. Each came to Arthur, looking him up and down while holding his hand. A procession of goodbyes unfolded, as knights, cowboys, werewolves, and even the dragon each bent low to his ears in the hopes that he would hear them.

They thanked him for his time, for his love and dedication. They thanked him for life, for their memories and loves. They thanked him for his attention and his persistence, for the comfort that they knew he would continue as long as he could.

Through her tears, Jillian understood. She could not believe, but she could accept.

She wondered if she was witnessing a dream, a miracle, or both.

Allister tapped her on the shoulder, offering her a gilded red-and-gold tissue.

All the while, Sam and Arthur both slept.

"Has everyone said what they need to?" Loki Crane asked.

Silence answered him.

"Then, perhaps it is time to leave our father with his greatest creation of all."

Loki Crane took his armored hand and gently lifted Sam's hand from over his folded book. Then, Loki Crane all too-softly lifted Arthur's hand as well. The room became darker and darker, as the characters faded from one world into countless others. One by one, they vanished.

Sam woke, bewildered. The lights in the room were bright. Arthur was awake, breathing heavily and smiling.

"Dad?" Sam asked. He stood from his chair, leaning his ear close to Arthur's mouth.

Arthur Ickes smiled, slowly moving a desperately weak arm to stroke his son's hair. From across the room, Jillian saw Arthur's mouth move, but could not hear his words.

Having finished what he needed to say, Arthur Ickes let his head fall and eyes close.

"Dad?"

**Author's Notes:** I was fortunate, in that my grandparents all lived into my adulthood. The night my grandfather died, I was with him. I wasn't with him the moment of his dying, but I was there a few hours before. I told him who I was, and that I was there. For the first time that night, he reached his hand up and I held it. I told him that I loved him, that we all loved him. And then I had to go.

Cancer is a horrible, awful thing. I don't wish it on my worst enemy, but it seems like these days everyone you meet has been affected by it. Someone's lost a mother, a father, or a child to cancer.

This story is dedicated to my Grandpa Ed and to my dad, who stepped up to that lonely role of the oldest son seeing his father off.

# Standing There

GHOSTS ARE SUPPOSED to haunt *old* places, yet here she is.

I walk out onto the patio, slide the glass door behind me and motion to crack open my beer before I turn around.

I've never thought being alone in the housing development would entail any sort of danger. We've been working on putting together this neighborhood for about a month now, and no one's run into any problems. As the foreman, I wanted to really get to know the property so I could tell my supervisors, who in turn would tell the future residents. Besides, I miss working with my hands, and being alone after I send my team home helps me think back.

And there she was.

She's standing in the living room behind me, where I'd just left a few seconds before.

She's looking at me so intensely that her eyes alone are enough to punch the air right out of my chest. They are wide and dark, full of the sort of excitement that people get when they are about to attack, an animal look of happiness that comes right before a fight. Her face is long, pulled in all directions so it's jagged and angular. Her skin is grey, as if it were drained and left underwater too long. Only the blood around her neck gives her any color, like a scarf so thick and thoroughly dark that I know it's blood only because it runs down in small raindrop streaks across her shirt.

She's tall. God, is she tall. She's standing almost to the ceiling now, looking at me and refusing to move.

Behind her, my cellphone is on a kitchen counter. Beyond her is the world, and she's between me and all of it.

I've been here for hours, paralyzed with fear and a growing fascination. Meanwhile, she has waved, as if she were made of plastic and air, or being carried by an invisible river-current. Her waist moves in a circle, her spine dancing like a snake every now and then while her legs shift in impossibly smooth and circular patterns.

I would think she was fake, a shadow magnified by exhaustion and lack of sleep; but, when I finally manage to muster the courage to go for the door, as my hand touches the handle, her smile grows wider. I remember hearing about wolves' smiles when I was just a kid, and my hand slowly comes away from the door.

Though I haven't looked at it, I know the sky is orange-purple now. The calls of the city are growing louder with nighttime traffic, but more distant as the darkness plays its tricks with my mind. She hasn't moved, save to waver and flitter in slow undulations. In the back of my mind, I *know* I am hungry. I *know* I need to pee. But these concerns seem so insignificant when compared to the overbearing dread that holds my feet still.

As the shadows extend she comes closer to the door. Soon, it is *her* hand on the handle. The glass comes open slowly, loudly. I back away, throwing myself against the fence, and command myself to scream. What comes out is nothing more than a dry whimper.

She shushes me, putting a long finger to her lips. Her hands are at my armpits, lifting me from the ground and to her face. She smiles softer now.

She opens her mouth wide, and I see what's inside.

Before I can scream, she kisses my neck away.

**Author's Notes:** At their most simple, and most terrifying, ghosts are unexplained encounters. Something, or someone, who wasn't there before. They don't always need a story, not to be scary. Indeed, the absence of a story often contributes to the unease. Why would this happen? Why there? This story was written on a whim, but remains one of my favorite little pieces of flash fiction.

# Christmas Alone

ASHLEY WENT FARTHER into the woods than her normal walks took her. Behind her were the white-covered fruits of her life's labor, the earned reward of hard work that filled her with writhing, nervous pride. The anxiety of her gleaning diploma and the increasingly claustrophobic office sent her flying from her house, into the looming woods, only armed with a jacket and an axe.

She darted, frantically searching for a purpose to keep her away and to justify her waste of time. Her family's impending visit swelled into a nightmare slideshow of hypotheticals as her eyes floated across every tree she saw. She gripped her axe handle tight, breathing in between hissing, cold breaths.

She stopped when she saw the tree, a small evergreen almost as tall as she was, standing alone and still in the midst of taller brothers. She squinted in the winter-noon darkness, wondering if it was the grey, cloudy sky that made the pine needles a darker, bluer shade. Around her the wind kicked up in whispers. She shook them off and raised her axe, just as her father had showed her all those winters ago.

Ashley hauled it back through the woods, straining herself beneath her layers as she heaved her body into an exhausted, ignorant nirvana. She brought it through her door wrapped in an old carpet and stood it on a cast-iron mount above her water dish. In the light of the house it was still dark, still permeating with a coldness that burned like fire as she scraped its bristles. She shook her head and decorated it in purple Christmas lights, humming a song she had never heard before as she placed each light with ceremonial precision.

Then she cleaned her house, doused every surface with disinfectant as she spiritually prepared herself for the looming visit. Ashley hadn't been home since she left for graduate school. Now that she landed an associate professorship which nearly tripled her income, she had plenty of space to host.

When they finally came, they liked everything...everything except for the tree.

Joey wouldn't touch it, refused to hang ornaments on it. Claimed that it stank, something that the brat would say just to get out of doing work, something that he *always* did. Dad frowned, flicked the needles and didn't say anything else. Mom reluctantly smiled and put the purple ornaments on the black-green needles slowly and carefully. She cried out, startled, and dropped one of the things to the floor, where it immediately shattered.

Her hand was bleeding; something had cut her deeply across the palm. Joey was freaking out, swearing and pointing at the tree in a fit of juvenile imagination. Ashley swore back, getting bandages and iodine while Dad calmly told everyone to just shut up for a minute.

There were no windows open on Christmas Eve, but the wind whispered throughout the hallways like the murmur of a slowly rising river. The scent of pine rode with it, forcing itself into the nose and nerves of those who inhaled it. There was an evil crawling sound slithering the hallways as everyone slept. There was splitting, screaming, and cheerful laughter across Ashley's little house.

But in the morning, everything was silent.

Everything was still.

The wind had stopped whispering, and the only scent left was that of a haunting. Ashley sat alone, in front of the tree decorated with purple ornaments and red blotches. The gifts below were gone, leaving a clean and clear view of the water dish she had so solemnly filled.

She had fulfilled her duty. The tree was different; it didn't need water at all.

It needed something else entirely.

And now she was spending Christmas alone.

**Author's Notes:** When I describe stories to my "normal" friends, this is always the one that gets the most laughs. A murderous Christmas tree? Come on. But a long time ago, there was a call for flash fiction from a certain respected magazine. *Weird Tales* enjoyed a brief online presence somewhere back in the early 2010s, and this was going to be my first published story. I was so thrilled, so excited to finally be a published author. When the magazine went under, and my story sat silent, I gave up writing entirely.

Or, I thought I did.

# Part II: Miskatonic and Mythos

# The Cthulhu Candidate

JENN HATED ELECTION years. She had become a reporter in part due to her childhood hero, Lois Lane. She would still loudly proclaim, over the rim of a margarita or a beer, that Lois didn't get the credit she deserved. Here was a Pulitzer Prize-winning journalist, here was an ace reporter who time and time again exposed scandals with earth-shattering exposés, and at best she was *saved* by Superman. At worst, she was his arm candy. His "baby momma."

Jenn felt the same way about election years that she did about Superman. It reduced what she was, a journalist who had been through warzones, coups, and congressional hearings, to a gossip columnist. What was each candidate wearing? What was their most damning soundbite? What did they eat at the Iowa State Fair?

Meanwhile, all the candidates had to do was smile and promise to save the world.

The newsroom was moving around her. There was a semi-blinding wall of lights, all pointed at her to make her desk boldly glow with the network's logo. Then there were the teleprompters and screens. One of her screens was off, as she had opted to turn off the teleprompter. She was fairly confident that this would be an easy interview. Another screen remained a solid shade of green, a satellite link that was blank because the congressman not yet prepped and linked for his interview.

Beyond these screens and lights, the dark silhouettes of technicians and producers floated around with clipboards, pacing nervously, on alert for any developments in this story or any other. Her executive producer Mike was prepping her through her earpiece.

"I think you can be as hard on this guy as you want." His voice was the same tone of perpetual exhaustion that they all spoke with in the newsroom, having stayed up all night researching the relatively unknown congressman. What they had found hardly let them sleep.

"The public and even his own party turned against him. Nobody wants this guy to run. Really, make that the focus and I think we'll have a show."

She nodded.

Someone behind the wall of lights held up the dark outline of a hand.

*Three. Two. One.*

"Good morning, I'm Jenn Mahnken. Today we're joined by Congressman Robert Marsh. Congressman, thank you for joining us."

"Please, Jenn. The pleasure is all mine."

Looking at the satellite feed, she could immediately see why people did not like the congressman. He had a wide face, with a long, jutting nose and cheeks that looked like they were being pulled towards his chest. His black hair was sparse, greying and dying atop too-white flesh the color of a glowing cave mushroom.

It was his eyes, though, that stuck out the most.

They were wide, some of the widest she had ever seen. And yet it seemed as if they were actually *further back* in his skull. The darkness around the eyes only made them unnaturally grey, giving rise to the rumor that the congressman was partially blind.

"Thanks for having me," he added in a high, nasally voice.

"Congressman," she began her interview, "tell me about your decision to run for president."

"Well, Jenn," he began, "I think that the American people, and certainly my constituents, are tired of politics-as-usual. Every year they seem to pick someone who leaves them behind. My hometown of Innsmouth, for example. Every year I go to my fellow congressmen and ask for any sort of help, whether it be in the form of a military base or reparations for the massacre of 1927 (which many of my fellow congressmen *still* refuse to acknowledge, by the way). But our jobs are going away, people are tired, and they just don't trust our government anymore. They don't trust the families that seem to be running it. Your Kennedys, your Bushes, your Clintons, your Trumps. I think the American people want *new blood* in their politics."

"Congressman, let's address that point first. You make a lot of criticism against what you've called 'nepotism,' but you yourself are from a powerful family in the Miskatonic region. Your family has a perhaps *equally* controversial history as the families you mention. How exactly is it that your position is different from theirs?"

The congressman nodded, smiling blandly and plainly. Jenn cringed inwardly, wanting to interview anyone but him.

"That's a great question, Jenn. You're right, the Marshes *are* pretty influential in the Miskatonic region. We've been called everything from 'fish-barons' to 'high priests.' But unlike these other families, we've always been outcast from the rest of 'high society.' Until recently, there had never been a Marsh in politics. I think that experience has kept us out of politics-as-usual, and our experience as outsiders has really influenced our perspective. Like most of America, we feel like we're looking in on our government from the outside of a window. And Jenn, we don't like what we see."

She watched the broadcast screen which they overlaid against the congressman. Pictures of Innsmouth, Massachusetts. Doing their research, her team was unsure how the town managed to stay out of constant limelight. Not only was it home to one of the largest temples of an extremely violent and notorious faith, but it had been the site of two government massacres. How do you hide something like that?

"Congressman, let's talk about your party affiliation. Which has been...marked, to say the least."

The congressman laughed in an almost neighborly tone.

"Yes, of course."

"You began your career as a Democrat, then a Republican. Currently you're an Independent. Reportedly, you've called yourself a self-avowed 'socialistic fascist' in private meetings with constituents. What exactly *are* your politics?"

"Well, you have to understand that politics, like all human things, is truly meaningless, Jenn."

There it was. The killer soundbite.

"I'm sorry, Congressman. Can you repeat that?"

"Well, Jenn. The goal of politics is to fight. Fight for your constituents, for what you believe in. For your principals and your interests. A political *party* is just a vehicle to this end. So, whatever I call myself, or whatever I run as, doesn't really matter. None of it does. All that matters is that I fight to best serve the interests of my constituents, and now, the American people."

"And let's talk about your constituents. Congressman, you are the first member of the United States government to be a member of the Esoteric Order of Dagon. What do you say to critics who view your religion as inherently antagonistic towards American values?"

"Jenn, let me clear up some misconceptions." The congressman licked his lips, his tongue purple and fat against his pale skin.

"First of all, I am hardly the 'first' member of my religion to serve in government. Indeed, many politicians, many *powerful* people have been members of the Esoteric Order of Dagon. Only, they haven't felt *comfortable* sharing their faith. We live in a remarkable time where people are becoming more accepting of each other. A truly beautiful thing. The more *accurate* statement would be that I am the first *open* member of the Esoteric Order of Dagon.

"Secondly, you are referencing the most recent attacks in Montreal and Beirut. What you should know is that these heinous and evil attacks were carried out by the Order of the Yellow Sign, *not* the Esoteric Order of Dagon. It's true that our faiths stem from a shared tradition, but if you bother to look into their histories, the Esoteric Order and the Yellow Sign are actually in a bitter, centuries-long conflict."

"That may be true, Congressman." She wondered if she should question him about how exactly he knew there were 'secret members' of his order in the U.S. government, if she should ask for specific names. She decided against it, continuing as she said, "But what I am *actually* referring to is your religion's emphasis on incest and human sacrifice."

"Those practices were banned in the early 1920s, almost one hundred years ago."

"That's...*considerably recent*, Congressman."

She hoped she wasn't smiling, but this was the sort of journalism she signed up for. The sort Ms. Lane would be proud of. The congressman seemed to balk for a moment, inhaling to make his expanded face bloat. She repressed a gasp, noticing how much he looked like a frog when he did this.

"I'll be the first to admit that horrible things have been done in the name of my faith, Jenn. But I'd hardly be the first. Governor Romney's religion came under scrutiny in 2012; our president has been lampooned for his involvement in a controversial church. I mean...goodness, Jenn." He motioned with his arms, as if he were making a profound point. "The entire effort to expand our nation was motivated in part by an idea to spread Christianity to Native Americans. In the process, we killed nearly all of them."

"Just to be clear, Congressman, I am referring to *strict doctrinal practices* of the Esoteric Order. The government raid you spoke about earlier, will you admit that this was carried out because residents of Innsmouth were found to be *sacrificing and mutilating* travelers?"

The congressman turned a shade red, the color of a starfish as it undulated sickly across the black ocean floor. He shook, apparently thinking that this would be some sort of cushier meet the press interview, the same sort of low-ball questions they forced reporters on the big two networks to do to create a fictitious "bias towards fairness." As if the truth was always fair.

Then, the congressman smiled. Jenn's blood ran cold. The way he smiled broke apart all of the anger in his expression, the façade of concern shattered downward, and revealed a new, darker layer. The congressman's teeth were jagged and pointed, long, narrow, and an unseemly shade of yellow in his wide mouth.

"Yes...yes, Jenn. That is what happened. Might I, however, defend some of the actions of my order?"

She was caught off guard. The sudden confidence which he presented himself with was unnerving, to say the least. The friendliness had peeled away, and in its stead was the presence of a man who clearly thought himself in control.

Unable to fully scrutinize his sudden change in demeanor, she opted to simply keep the interview going.

"Of course, Congressman." Her voice was weak, weaker than it had been in Iraq or Afghanistan; weaker than it had been when she interviewed warlords and terrorists. There was something outside of her control, something imposing an unnatural-yet-reflexive fear.

The congressman seemed to know this, and when he laughed it was not in the high-pitched falsetto he had used before. The laugh was low and guttural, dark, dirty water bubbling up from miles beneath the surface. The skin on his face rippled and shook like the surface of disturbed waters.

"Jenn, the men and women who came to Innsmouth weren't what you would call *intelligent* people. They were warned at every possible turn to escape, to avoid the place, that the town became different at night. Jenn...you've seen horror movies, yes? *Those* are the people you lost, the sort that open the door knowing full damn well that there are consequences behind them. Ask your average moviegoer and they'll tell you that they think those characters *deserve* what's coming to them. So, no, I am not sure that the Esoteric Order truly ever committed sins worth crying about.

"The other thing you should consider is that outsiders believe they are somehow *different*." The scenery behind the congressman flickered from a shot of the Massachusetts state capital to something else. For five seconds she clearly saw something that she could not identify. Towers with weird, jutting angles, encircled by dark skies with debris and dust swirling through them. The screen flickered back, and the congressman stood before the state capital.

Beyond the wall of lights, she heard her producers panicking in the darkness, unsure of what had gone wrong with the signal to present such a disturbing image. The congressman, either unaware or unbothered by this disturbance, continued speaking:

"What you should consider is that you are not that different from us *at all*. Prior to the return of Obed Marsh, our community was starving. In poverty, our residents were too poor to move. So, our ancestors turned to something far greater than themselves in an attempt to save their lives and those of their children.

"Should you ever become so desperate, you will be surprised at what you can do. Already we know that humanity coalesces around demagogues when it is scared, when it is tired and hungry and jumping at its own shadows. Even at the expense of its freedoms, it will do so. The only difference between your demagogues and our *gods* is that ours provide *results*, but time and time again yours do not."

Jenn's teleprompter, turned off at the start of the interview, was now alive with red script. The machine was not capable of producing the color red, nor was it capable of producing the dripping, bloody font that the words were written in. Words she had never seen before:

"*Ph'nglui mglw'nafh Cthulhu R'lyeh wgah'nagl fhtagn.*"

Could she even call them words?

She waited for Mike's voice in her earpiece, telling her the system had been hacked.

"Congressman." She tried to find her words. "We seem to be experiencing some technical difficulties—"

"No, Jenn. It only *seems* that way because you're beginning to get a view of the world as it truly is."

When she heard the voice in her earpiece speak, it wasn't Mike's.

"Keep the signal going. Keep talking."

The congressman's voice was low and gravelly in her ear.

She froze. In the darkness behind the lights, the crew seemed to *shamble* rather than *walk*. Two dark shapes collided with each other, clipboards and papers falling to the floor with loud, shattering sounds. An indistinct meld of gurgles began to fill the air, and Jenn felt her skin going cold and her mind slipping quickly. While the congressman continued to speak via the satellite connection, his voice in her ear whispered:

"You're doing great, Jenn. Just a *little longer.*"

There was a low, evil amusement there. If sharks could speak, they would not sound all-too different from Congressman Robert Marsh.

"I think that Americans have always been aware of the truth of this world. Maybe that's part of the reason our country has fought for so long and so hard to define itself, to make itself 'great.' I think when the pilgrims first landed on Plymouth Rock that there was something wholly insignificant in the moment. They had merely transplanted themselves from one 'oppressive' part of the planet to another. They knew, because they had to know, that all they were could be summed up in one word: dust."

The congressman's voice in her earpiece began a chant.

She screamed and grabbed the piece, sending it hurtling towards the floor beneath her desk and shattering it with the crunch of an empty locust shell. She cautiously looked back at the screen, once more seeing the congressman standing before those twisted spires and dark skies.

He was paler against this backdrop, his eyes wider and greyer. Long, needle-like teeth protruded from his fat lips. His hair fell away, revealing patches of dry skin that flaked and gleamed like fish-scales. His blind eyes pierced Jenn's mind, probing into the dark places where she had before been able to successfully overcome and repress her fears. Now, her mind was barely able to form the silent words of thoughts.

"I am campaigning on a promise, Jenn. And that promise is simple. I will *deliver.* I will fulfill *every single one* of my promises, because I am going to fulfill them *now.*"

Behind the congressman something moved between the spires, a shadow darker and more ominous than the sky it stood against. The shadow turned towards the camera with glowing yellow eyes and Jenn could not control her screams.

"I promise to give the people of this world exactly what they deserve. I promise that I will allow them to fulfill the only true function that they ever had. You know," he chuckled, "there was a recent poll that suggested that Americans would rather be wiped out by a meteor than vote for the top two candidates. Well, I can give you something even better."

Jenn thrashed on the floor. Above her the studio lights were shaking, beneath her the earth shifting. From beyond the studio walls, the screams of millions overtook her own. The congressman continued to speak, his voice rising above every other sound:

"This country was never great. This *world* was never great. But Great Cthulhu is coming. Mother Hydra. Father Dagon. Iä! Iä! Shub-Niggurath!"

His voice descended from words into twisting chants. For hours he continued, until he finally spoke again:

"Jenn, I want to thank you for having me on. The media has always been a great help in creating candidates, in giving attention to something that they shouldn't. For decades your government tried so hard to censor and hide us. Who would have imagined that the best way to get all of these eyes on us was to come on board for an interview?

"We should have thought of it earlier; the media gives platforms to *anyone!*"

After that, she didn't hear the congressman for much longer. Above her stood a shadow without a face. And though the shadow had no face, in the swinging lights of the studio she could see that it *did* have a mouth.

And the mouth opened wide.


**Author's Notes:** This story became something of a cult hit, and it was one of the hardest ones to not include in *Whiskey and Other Unusual Ghosts*. Its biggest champion has been fellow author Alan Sessler, who even made an animated music video about the congressman (who bears a striking resemblance to a certain alleged serial killer and confirmed senator) that can be found on his YouTube channel, Alan Postscript.

We all see the meme every year: "Cthulhu (INPUT YEAR HERE): why vote for the lesser evil?" I suppose that's where the inspiration came from, though it wasn't conscious. Congressman Marsh was supposed to be a one-off, a funny satire that was rushed into inclusion before the election of 2016. But repeatedly, current events inspired a reaction in me, and Congressman Marsh became part of how I processed those reactions. Because of this, his stories became less funny and far more serious. What began life as a fun way to lampoon American politics, presidential elections, and the media became the character I used to explore the very real danger posed by individual leaders who can damage institutions, incite violence, and inspire fear in people.

# Office Hours and After

I

THE FIRST VIGIL for Trevor Thomas was held the night after they found his corpse.

I didn't have any candles, hadn't thought to buy any, but my roommate left a scented lilac one before she left. It was a big, wide thing that I cautiously lit and cradled with both hands. I checked myself in the mirror: purple scarf, black hoodie, gloves. It was December in New England, and though it hadn't yet snowed, there was a biting chill blowing its way from the north. When the wind hit you, it felt like you were being cut into ribbons.

I cradled the candle and walked out of the dorm.

Campus had been quiet since they found his body. Trevor was discovered in the bushes outside of the Department of Ancient History, his hands bound behind his back, his mouth gagged, and his ribcage wide open for all the world to see. On his stomach, beneath the gaping wound along his chest, Miskatonic University PD found an intricate symbol: a nine-pointed star associated with the "alignment" that would wake Cthulhu from its slumber.

They hadn't found him until the morning after his murder. There were probably screams; how couldn't there have been? They had found a pool of blood in a department hallway, indicating that the murder had begun in the building before the killer dragged the body outside. But every campus police officer had been at the Esoteric Order of Dagon the night Trevor died, trying to deal with the protests and counter-protests brought on by a visit by Congressman Marsh.

A wind rushed up and bit my exposed cheeks and nose, roaring as if from the vacuum between the stars. I felt the blood run to my face and gulped back something sour. Despite the cold, it was important that I be there. I hadn't come to Miskatonic to make friends or have relationships, a pronouncement that I wore on my sleeve as prominently as possible. I had a way of making the air colder around me, a way of silencing people with an icy stare before they could even begin their small talk. Some people, boys really, still tried talking to me. I was pretty, after all, a fact that made people even more disdainful of my outspoken disinterest in them. But my defenses normally kept anyone who wanted anything from me away. It didn't make me popular, but again, I didn't want to be. Instead, I just wanted all the time I could to study. To delve into every secret Miskatonic could offer.

The nickname—"Loathsome" Laura Nodens—came from the girls, and the boys called me the "Wallflower Witch." To tell the truth, I actually quite liked both. The tendency of people to distance and shun what they couldn't understand made me smile.

But that wasn't the case with Trevor. My first quarter at Miskatonic, Trevor had been one of my TAs. Over the winter break, he caught me eating alone in the dining hall and sat across from me without asking. My eyes did not scare him away, the cold air did not make him uneasy or nervous, and I realized he didn't want anything from me other than to see if I was okay. He didn't stay long after I explained that my home was a bit too far away to go back to, just nodded and said to feel free to come by his office hours next semester if I needed any help with classes.

Curiosity overtook me, and despite myself, I made a friend. Albeit not a *great* friend, not a particularly *close* friendship, but Trevor had become something of a mentor of mine. His death was hard on me, and I wanted to make sure that everyone understood who, exactly, Miskatonic had lost.

To my relief and delight, the quad was alive with small, sparking flames. Orange stars wavered and blew in the turning wind. Trevor's smiling face beamed out from poster boards, framed by cards and sticky notes explaining how much he was loved and how much he was missed. His students whispered how good of a teacher he was; his teachers responded that he was a good student too. Solemnly, they asked each other about his family, about his girlfriend and parents.

People, for all their inane stupidity, could be profoundly kind.

And it was because of this simple, inexplicable kindness that I pledged to find Trevor's killer.

## II

One of the perks of being "loathsome" is that I scared my roommate away pretty early.

The poor girl hadn't really understood why she felt nauseous every night or why she always smelled rotting eggs in the morning. She had awful nightmares, too, things that sent her reeling from her mattress and screaming as if she was being torn into with a jagged stone knife. She finally went back home to Boston, and I understand from campus gossip that the family believed she had a nervous breakdown.

Perfectly explainable. After all, *I* had no nightmares, and *I* never thought the room smelled particularly bad.

But after she left, the room was mine. I covered the walls with blank butcher-paper canvases. For all the mystique around blood and "vital fluids," Sharpies do just fine for drawing symbols. Elder Signs and pentagrams interwove to form a complicated hieroglyphic algebra that covered every surface of my room. There were spells for virtually everything I could think of: for entering my own dreams, for keeping out things from beyond.

At the moment, however, I only needed a door.

I sat cross-legged on the floor of my room and focused on a rectangle interwoven with circles and jutting, angular lines. I squinted and held my breath for as long as I could, letting the room fade to darkness and exploding stars before my lungs gave in, and I breathed, quickly reaching for the symbol and opening the portal.

My destination was not far away, and I would only have to travel in the space-between for a few moments. That said, I frowned as I entered the domain of the Outer Gods, greeted by their howling jeers.

The infernal chorus roared as I fell, screaming obscenities in the tongues of Lemuria and Atlantis, calling me everything but my name. I laughed in response, and the force of my voice was enough to quiet their bleating and trumpeting, so they would focus their attention more carefully on the pale object streaming across their realm. By the time they realized what I was, I was already where I needed to be, well beyond their domain.

MUPD.

Officers in their too-formal blue uniforms darted from one room to the next, piles of manila folders and papers in their hands. Nervous eyes darting from sleepless sockets, pale flesh covered in sweat that stank of stale coffee and sleepless panic. A cacophony of swears, ringing telephones, and angry shouting. One voice boomed, another cried. An officer consoled a young woman who claimed (lied) that she had seen the murder. Another officer drafted a statement to the press, muttering obscenities under his breath as he imagined stepping in front of the cameras.

In my astral form, I couldn't be seen. In this form, I was more sensitive to their thoughts, an ethereal and telepathic sponge if I let myself be. I faded into the background, seeping into the cracks in the walls as minutes became hours. As I crept into their minds, I realized that none of them had the true picture, though some of them knew far more than they should. Some had been bribed by faculty for their silence; others had witnessed ancient rites. Still others had blood on their hands—evil men with soft smiles and friendly faces. And all of them burned with thoughts of Trevor Thomas, of the riots during Congressman Marsh's visit.

National attention was on the University again, and they needed to find answers fast before a panic started and the governor sent in the National Guard. It had happened once before, in the 1970s when that Whateley kid had been murdered by a faculty member.

Arkham hadn't been the same since.

I hummed to myself and let their thoughts pour into me—collecting everything they knew.

Even what they wouldn't tell each other.

When I had what I needed, I launched myself back through the void between the worlds, now silent. They wouldn't dare taunt me now that they could recognize me for what I was. Unadorned of flesh, they only bowed in reverence.

The eyes of my body opened wide as breath filled my lungs.

It was a matter of finding enough blank space between my symbols. I wrote down every name, every fact that I had absorbed while projecting into the police station. There was the Esoteric Order of Dagon; it was one of their symbols that was carved into Trevor's stomach after all. It wasn't known if Trevor had any contact with the order, but apparently a few of their more zealous members had become more aggressive in the wake of the congressman's visit. Human sacrifice wasn't a stretch, though they had publicly abandoned the practice in the late 1940s.

Then there were his fellow graduate students in the department. Miskatonic was known for attracting some of the most brilliant scholars in the world, and the graduate students were no exception. But they were famous for their infighting, cutthroat young scholars vying for grants that were becoming scarcer every year. Grad students regularly suffered bouts of nausea, hallucinations, and vertigo that made them miss important deadlines. Weeks later, they would find someone had slipped poison into their coffee or a symbol under their mattress. It wasn't difficult to imagine one Miskatonic graduate student killing another, either out of jealousy or simply to reduce competition. After all, it had happened before.

I sighed. The pool of suspects was already wide. There were hundreds of graduate students, and if the motive of Trevor's killers was simply to reduce competition, it could be any of them. University grants could go to any department, and outside funding was even more nebulous and ambiguous. In ancient history alone, there were fifty graduate students of various rank and progress. If I was going to look into them, I would need to begin with his cohorts.

I wrote ten names on the wall. I knew three of them, TAs I had my freshman year. I hadn't cared for any of them, all of them typically snide and hateful toward undergraduates.

Then there was Professor Arthur Richards. The police believed he may be a suspect, though they hoped not. Dr. Richards had been accused in the past of involving his research assistants in ancient rites, of performing secret rituals on his students without their knowledge or consent. The rumor had been, in fact, why I took one of his seminars my first semester at Miskatonic. But the old man was a fool without even enough knowledge to be dangerous.

The last group of suspects came from Omega House. They were a powerful fraternity, and one that Trevor had an apparent falling out with after a few of the brothers plagiarized on their final paper. The story MUPD told was that he had complained to the dean about receiving pressure from Omega leadership to look the other way. The Omegas were a bad lot: just the right mix of typically attractive, intelligent, and hot-headed to also be cruel and reckless. It didn't help that the Omegas' pockets ran deep into the undercurrent of wealth beneath Arkham. In virtually every market, illegal and otherwise, the Omegas' tendrils spread far and wide. There was a joke, whispered only off-campus and behind closed doors, that the Omegas were "the Illuminati in training."

All of that said, they would be the easiest.

I'd start with them first.

But Trevor had died, and despite myself, thoughts of his death were weighing on my mind. I stretched, rising from the floor and sighing loudly. Looking into the mirror, I saw the day had been harder on me than I thought. Disheveled hair, dim eyes. I sometimes needed to remind myself that bodies had limits, that if I wasn't careful I would break mine.

I slipped into cool sheets and sang myself songs of Kadath. As the melody became a soft whisper, I launched myself beyond the wall of sleep, enveloped in the arms of those who knew me once before.

### III

The Omega brothers were awful, foul people. Smug, vain things who hid the knowledge of their own smallness behind smiles and vestments of power. They attempted to dominate every room they entered, and it was perhaps for that reason more than any other that Omegas so frequently clashed with Trevor.

Trevor Thomas had a booming voice, one that filled the room when he spoke. He had a wild smile and a stage presence that the best professors and lecturers took years to master. I remembered a moment when he had kicked a group of brothers out for talking loudly in discussion.

"*We'll go to the administration with this bullshit,*" they had screamed at him.

"*I'm looking forward to it,*" he yelled back.

We all laughed.

Looking in the mirror, I saw my smile. Reflexively, I resumed my normal expression and brushed my hair. The Omegas would be easy enough to get information out of, but it wouldn't hurt to be outwardly charming either. Before anything, the Omegas were boys aspiring to be men, stupid little kids only partially aware of what they were and frantically trying to be anything else.

A slim-fitting black dress. Soft pink lipstick. Diamond earrings.

I held my pendant in my hand, wondering if I should leave it. It was a simple, inconspicuous thing that only the trained eye or upmost initiate would recognize; nothing but a triangle circumscribed by a circle.

When I wore it above my clothes, I only received innocent, naive questions as to which Harry Potter character was my favorite. It would be nothing to leave it behind.

But it is one of the few things I have that reminds me of who I am. Of *what* I am.

I slipped it beneath my dress, relieved in the knowledge that it was there.

Then came the oils, the perfumes. Incantations for Shub-Niggurath. For Yog-Sothoth. For blind, nuclear Azathoth. I surveyed myself in the mirror. I smiled and pretended to laugh.

The Omegas would be easy.

The house was a faux-Greek monolith, its symbol attempting to invoke a feeling of doom and futility. The long porch was lined with pillars where members drew symbols in spray paint, sharpies, and blood. One of the thousands of symbols, none of which the brothers properly understood, kept out astral forms. But the Omegas themselves let everyone in, smiling as they surveyed the line of partygoers who sought for a moment to get away from their stress and studies.

Inside, the house was lit only by dim neon-purple lights; loud music thumped and warm bodies pushed against each other in a haze of sweat and alcohol. I felt the eyes on me, the eyes that would give me power. This sort of magic was easy and cheap, usually beneath me.

A red plastic cup came into my hand, beer that tasted like warm, bubbly water. I drank it with a smile and a flash of my eyes. I snaked my way across the dance floor, weaving ornate patterns of legs and arms, my blood alive and hot. For a moment, I forgot myself and enjoyed it. For a moment, I wondered how great it would be to follow them into reckless abandon, to leave myself behind and wade into the alcohol and the hum of the bass. For a moment, the vibrations flowed through me better than any dream song.

And then I caught their eyes.

The brothers Trevor had kicked out of his class.

They probably didn't recognize me; I have ways of making people's eyes drift when I want. But now I had them, and when I flashed my teeth, I knew their hearts were palpitating. I could make them feel what they truly were.

Children.

A few playful laughs, a slow trace up one of their shoulders.

I suggested to one, the one who had so rudely shouted that he would go to the administration over Trevor, that we go upstairs. He gulped, and I laughed, leading him by the hand and telling him that I wanted to talk. That the music was too loud.

I walked him slowly, teasingly past the crowds who wooed and clapped. Hands came down on his back, red cups went up.

I opened a door and led him through, a mattress on the ground and a mess of sheets and swimsuit model posters.

"Tell me about Trevor Thomas," I said, locking the door behind us.

His face went from an anxious smile to a dumbfounded, blank expression.

"What?" was all he could manage.

The lights around us dimmed.

I looked at my hand, impatiently waiting. The lights flickered again. Behind me, a bulb shattered and burst.

He jumped, his shoulders lurching as his eyes widened.

"Oh God, it's *you!*" He made a motion for the door, and I let him fall into my eyes. He froze, breath quivering and sweat gathering. Around us, darkness rose, and the shadows began to roar. With my palm, I slowly and softly pushed his chest, sending him toppling onto his mattress so I could stand over him.

His eyes shifted away from me and toward the darkness at my back.

Growling rose all around us.

He was getting paler by the second.

"Don't look at them. Look at me. You'll just make them nervous."

But he couldn't look away. I brought the back of my hand swiftly across his face. It reddened and bled. Rage pooled into his eyes and voice.

"You *bitch*," he said, with all the vitriol of someone who considered it a powerful word. "Do you know who I am?"

"Ricky Baker, senior, business major. You're going to inherit quite a bit of money, and everyone knows that. But what most don't know is what you did to that girl, Ricky." I leaned down so that my face was level to his. A long black tendril came from the darkness behind me and wrapped itself gingerly around his neck.

He reached for it only to have it tighten slightly. He frantically shook his head.

I hated him more than ever. Egotistical, assessing his life as worth saving. But he was little more than a stain on the universe, and a malignant one at that. As tears welled in his eyes, I decided that I may end him one day.

But not then. Not when I just wanted him to talk.

"Tell me about Trevor Thomas. The Omegas weren't fans of his. Know anything about his death?"

He trembled, unresponsive, gaze shifting from me to the growing void behind.

I smiled. "Maybe I should tell you a little about what's back there. How many eyes? How many teeth?" He looked back at me, mouth falling open. "Maybe I should tell you that everything you've read is wrong. That you could not possibly know, no book could possibly *tell* you, how much it hurts being torn apart. That no writer, Al-Hazred or otherwise, knew how *long* they spend playing with their food before they eat it. I'll give you to them, Ricky. I *will*. Your life doesn't mean anything to me. So tell me what I want to know, and you get to live the rest of your natural life. Don't, and you'll live for days... months, maybe years. But it won't be pleasant, I promise."

He gagged up a choking, wet sob. Real fear—for the first time in his life, he was feeling it.

"Just breathe, Ricky. Just talk to me."

"W-we," he stammered, "had nothing to do with it."

"How do I know that? What if it was another brother, not you?"

"We knew the protest was going to happen, that there was probably gonna be a riot. We wanted e-e-everyone on lockdown! To avoid the news."

The tendril at his neck tightened, and another came from the darkness to hover above his face.

A scream died in his throat.

"I could check that, Ricky. If I found out you were lying...I'd *kill* you."

"I'm not! I'm not! Oh God."

The tendril left a red, burning mark as it unwrapped itself from his neck and retreated back into the darkness. The lights returned slowly. The noises of the party drifted through thin walls, happy shouting and the thrum of music.

I went for the door.

"Is that it?" he asked in a voice between relief and panic.

I gave him one last, sly look. "Not quite. You'll wake up from nightmares each morning for years. You'll wake up screaming, writhing in your own mess. But when you realize that you deserve those nightmares...that's when you'll *really* hurt, Ricky."

I left Ricky sobbing into his pillow. Behind me, the party continued as normal, and already people were forgetting I was ever there.

## IV

The Department of Ancient History had an open forum about Trevor's death, what it would mean for the department and its students. The lecture hall was packed with distraught and disinterested students, those who hung on their professors' every word alongside those who idly played with their phones. I sat in the back, examining the speakers as carefully as I could while surveying the crowd below.

Professor Richards was more charismatic than I remembered, speaking with a booming voice and waving hands. He was a tenured faculty member, known for his seminal volume *The Primordial Leng: The Rise and Fall of Pre-Human Civilization*. The book had established him as a name in the field, and because of it he was cited in virtually every book and article that came out of the Antarctic discovery. But the professor had gotten old, and his relevance was fading along with his greying beard and thinning hair.

In front of those young students though, he was alive. He spoke of Trevor's intense interest in shoggoths, his research into the Mi-Go folklore of northern Vermont. He recalled fondly mentoring Trevor, taking him in as an integral member of his research group. I could hear the crying rise from the students who were realizing (for perhaps the first time) that Trevor was more than just their TA.

As the students cleared, wiping their eyes and slinging their phones back into their pockets, I waited behind, resolved to be the last.

Dawn, my TA for Pre-Human Warfare, seemed nervous when she saw me. Most people were uneasy around me, and Dawn was no exception. She was twenty-four and had already acquired a lifetime of bitterness. Long blonde hair tied in a ponytail, pointed green eyes that leaked condescension and scorn. Her students knew she was intelligent, but she kept her knowledge guarded, driving office visitors away with terse and angry answers to even the friendliest of questions.

"Hi, Laura." Her voice was frantic, desperate to be anywhere else.

"Hi," I responded flatly.

"Was...Trevor a TA of yours?"

"My first semester, he gave me some feedback on my paper on the Yig Mounds. I visited him in office hours a lot, and he always encouraged me to speak up in class. I was hoping I'd get to have him as a TA again..."

"Yeah." Dawn's eyes drifted toward her watch. "We were working on a project with Professor Richards. He was brilliant, and I'll admit it made me a little jealous."

"No reason to be jealous. You graduate students are chronically hard on yourselves."

Arthur Richards had a ruddy complexion, reddened with the strain of standing longer than he was used to. He was a big man, wide in shoulder and stomach with a barreled chest that belonged to a former wrestler. Brown eyes shone dimly from under his glasses as he reached out to extend his hand to mine.

"Have I had you in one of my lectures?"

"Yes, Professor. My first semester. Trevor was my TA."

"Ah, yes. Of course! Well," his face became solemn, "we are all deeply saddened at his loss. We are coming to know he meant a great deal to our undergraduates. I've referred so many to campus services in the wake of his murder."

"I'm going somewhere next to talk to someone."

"Very good. Well, I apologize, but"—he placed a hand on Dawn's shoulder, and she jumped—"we need to leave. There is a meeting within the department, but please feel free to come to my office hours if you would like to talk more."

"Of course, Professor."

I watched Dawn and the professor leave the room. I have always been fascinated by the responses mankind can muster against adversity, against its own looming doom. The professor seemed to have found new energy, new life in a need to be strong for those around him. Meanwhile, Dawn was unsure and more than a little anxious. Guilt? Maybe. But then I thought of how she jumped at the professor's touch. Maybe there was something going on there, something taboo or even criminal.

I slung my backpack over my shoulder and walked out into the winter.

The dead yellow grass was littered with brown leaves. Each building was nearly uniform in design, commissioned in deliberate sequence by the wealthy heirs of Mayflower colonists who kept their family trees in gilded frames to show visitors. White roofs, narrow windows, and brown bricks loomed from every side. Every now and then, there was something particularly obtrusive, a building that was out of line with the others because a donor had insisted upon it.

Such was the Temple of the Esoteric Order of Dagon, a lightning rod for periodic controversy.

The temple was a sleek black mess of tall spires and red-stained windows. I thought it was laughable when I first saw it, a child's drawing of an evil lair, the Sagrada Familia made miniature and menacing. Walking up the obsidian steps, I was overtaken by the sea smell that wafted from inside. On the doors, a metal emblem of "Great" Cthulhu rested, its tentacles pouring out of a circle and resting just above the handles.

I snorted and pushed inward.

There were no visitors, no souls in the black cathedral, only quiet rows of pulpits lined with shells and scales. Red hymnals full of raving, nonsensical script rested on the purple cushions, a testament to the order's conflicting desires to appear both modern and ancient. Both comparable to and above other faiths.

Out of boredom, I lifted one of the hymnals and inhaled its musty smell.

"Can I help you, young lady?"

There was a tall, ghostly man whose dark skin only barely concealed the skeleton beneath. He wore a black robe adorned in emerald tentacles, rising from the frills of his robe like flames. His face told me that I had already won, that he had underestimated me and would soon tell me everything that I wanted to know.

I reached under the neck of my shirt and revealed my pendant. He peered, stooping his neck and narrowing his eyes. I walked closer and he gasped, his eyes moving from the pendant to my face.

"My apologies. Follow me into my office, and we'll talk."

I nodded, letting my feet slap the floor behind his as we calmly walked toward the back of the cathedral.

"How's Providence this time of year? Are you bringing new wisdom today?" He was eager, a child barking at the heels of their teacher.

"Not today."

"Hrm."

At the head of the chapel, aquatic sculptures stood proud and golden. The half-fish, half-man depiction of Dagon consuming a human torso; Mother Hydra birthing a legion of angler fish; Cthulhu, rising above the waves. I repressed my scoffing and followed the deacon into his office. I sat across from him at his desk, and he poured wine into a chalice, no doubt a gift that had been brought to him from the depths of some sunken Spanish galleon. It was sweet and sour on my tongue, unusual and alluring.

"If not to impart your starry wisdom, why are you here this day, sister?"

I sipped the wine again. "I wanted to ask if any of your members were involved in the murder of Trevor Thomas."

He shook his head. "No, we weren't."

"No one wanted to give the congressman a human sacrifice for his visit?"

"Plenty wanted to, yes. But I stepped in." He leaned back in his chair and inhaled, preparing to give a speech he had given before. One that he probably rehearsed in front of the mirror. "Earthly politics is a tool, a vehicle for power—little more. And such overt activities limit our ability to use this tool effectively. It cuts off our ability to channel and broadcast our message, no?"

I resisted the urge to roll my eyes. Before I could respond, he continued, words he had no doubt spoken thousands of times before.

"Don't you believe that all will be resolved when Great Cthulhu rises from the sea? When the oceans run red and we, the anointed and initiated, are left to claim the remaining lands for our gods?"

I finished my glass and placed it before me. I hated this, and I wanted him to know it.

"I think that 'believers' are just as likely to die with 'non-believers.'"

His mouth hung open. Surely, the Cthulhu cult would have accepted the inevitably that its members would be food just like the rest of mankind. Yet every time I gave this speech, they were surprised. I smiled, taking pleasure in imparting my truth.

"There's nothing special about 'Great' Cthulhu, and your order practices exactly the sort of politics that you seem to disdain. There is truth in your message, yes, sure. Maybe you can sing it to yourself when the Great Old Ones are flaying your flesh for all eternity. Maybe you'll take comfort that you were right about the screaming, searing void that you were so eagerly rushing toward."

I rose, annoyed and impatient. The deacon's mouth gaped, stuttering and frightened.

I left the temple as knowledgeable as when I entered.

V

At 3 a.m., the door to Wilmarth Hall was wide open. I braced myself, thinking of what half-truth excuse a sophomore could give a police officer as to why she followed them after hours. Walking through the door, I was reminded that the hall had been locked down for a few days now.

It was still an active crime scene, with yellow police tape still up. The blood had been cleared away, but I could still smell the lingering, bitter death. It gleamed, too pristine, too clean for a hall that most students walked through at least once during their Miskatonic career. In the night, abandoned, it seemed more like a catacomb and less like a lecture hall.

There was a crash above me, on the second floor. A long, metallic grating sound and the shattering of glass, a scream that mingled with the soft roar of radio static. Then silence.

I smiled.

My shoes slapped the stairs, loud and deliberate. But the sounds resumed, too taken up in their panic and despair to notice me. A short walk in a dark hallway, and I found myself at the TA offices, a place I had spent many hours, talking with Trevor.

The place where, I now knew, my friend had died.

Opening the door, I saw a shadow. It threw scattered papers into the air and howled in gurgling despair. My stomach dropped, dreading that some fool had actually unleashed a shoggoth on campus. But then the static-filled scream subsided, the arms stopped writhing, and I heard a distinctly human sob. The form fell to the floor, collapsing on its knees among the tossed papers.

In the pale moonlight that shone through the one open window, Professor Arthur Richards curled his fists into his beard. He turned slowly toward me, eyes narrowed and teeth bared. And then I knew.

I had been a fool, thinking Trevor's killer was human.

I kept quiet, letting him get a look at me before he spoke. He'd try to explain himself. His kind always tried to explain themselves.

He smiled with glinting, white teeth. "I see your necklace now."

I didn't respond. He laughed, pleased with himself.

"You probably just wanted to see what you could find. You never were looking for me, were you?"

"I would have been if I had known what I was looking for."

"Heh." He stooped now, lumbering toward me in long, striding steps.

"When did Trevor figure it out?" I asked.

"Oh, almost at the beginning. I am afraid he knew Professor Richards too well. The boy actually *cared* about the professor. Unlike so many others who only cared about his work. The poor boy actually had a heart." His smile was breaking his face. "I had to cut it out."

I stood my ground, not turning or running away from him.

"That's what I never understood about the Yithians. Why dissect things? Why take them apart when you already know how they work?"

He stood over me, lowering his head to mine. "For fun."

He lifted me up by my armpits and slammed me into a chalkboard. The metal shelf jammed into my back, shooting fire across my spine. In reflex, I screamed, biting on my lower lip and tasting the coppery tang of my blood. He held me there, his face so close that it bristled against mine.

"What is strange to me," he continued as his hand moved down to clasp my pendant, "is that I did not see that you would find me. I suppose the Crawler's witches have found how to conceal themselves from precognition."

Now it was my turn to smile.

My turn to laugh.

"Not...one of its witches."

He leaned down, chuckling. "What is that, girl?"

"Not one of its witches. One of its *aspects*."

I revealed myself, unfolding my flesh and allowing my form to seep through the thin veil between worlds. My thousand mouths poured from behind the shadows, my eyes leering from every corner. Around the room, I began to sing as I overtook that small patch of the universe. It had been so long since I'd shot off from my original form, since I had sent the Laura-aspect into this reality to probe and accumulate, that I had forgotten the satisfaction of being whole. In ecstasy, I unfolded, clawed tendrils and piping nostrils spilling from the walls in heaps of dark, piling flesh.

The Yithian screamed, falling onto his hands. I fell and watched him scramble to pull himself back up. I stabbed into him with a sharpened tendril, piercing through his chest and lifting him into the air. He spilt his gore out on the floor, choking and sobbing.

"Please—"

A clawed arm tore into his chest, feeling the spot where his heart was.

His screams became wet whimpers.

The Yithian whispered for mercy in its native language, a pre-human tongue that I knew all too well.

But it was too late. I had forgotten how it felt to be together, having been separated for so long. I resolved that I would not go apart hungry.

I pulled him toward a wide, gaping mouth.

Passing a human body was always painful.

Luckily, I wouldn't be doing it with just one stomach.


**Author's Notes:** Laura Nodens is an autobiographical character, as is Trevor Thomas. In college I was terrified of drinking, because I believed that it would mean the total destruction of myself. I was a reluctant kid, and became a reluctant adult. The idea of losing control of my person truly scared me.

So the character of Laura began there, and then developed into someone of an "uncertain self." Who is this person? *What* are they? Trevor Thomas was me, as a teacher. You try to do good and care about your students, but sometimes they just fall off.

The story remains one of my favorites and was one of my very first pro sales. A big thank you to Scott Gable for publishing it.

# The Referendum Over Innsmouth

IT WAS LIBERATING when he learned God didn't care.

It didn't matter that he never finished his degree, or that he was almost universally shunned by everyone he met. It didn't matter that he made women uneasy, or that he kept odd hours at shit jobs.

If God didn't care, why should he?

It was a blank check.

Better than unconditional love, it was *cosmic indifference.*

That's why, when he learned about the Innsmouth Refurbishment Project, he knew he had to do something. They were erasing history, building over something terrifying and awe-inspiring so they could be comfortable pursuing an impossible feel-good future. He'd spent countless hours on the forums, pouring his outrage into chatrooms full of like-minded people.

How dare they?

How *dare* they?

A few of them, those who truly believed, posted an advertisement for a rally in Innsmouth to preserve the town's historic significance. He didn't follow or care for politics, but he'd remembered the name "Congressman Marsh" with some passing curiosity. Searching the congressman's presidential campaign website, he found enough to like.

The bus to Innsmouth was full of all sorts of people. The driver didn't have "the look," the wide-eyed gaze that saw farther into the truth than any man could. Instead, he was an obese older man, probably Honduran, who gave him and everyone else on the bus dirty looks as they boarded. He sat between some woman dully looking at her phone and a man in a turban shoveling an order of Indian food into his mouth with a plastic fork.

He let out a sigh of relief when the bus came to Innsmouth, pushing past the sneezing, coughing masses and out into the damp New England air. He'd never been to Innsmouth, too scared and too hurt after he read about what happened to the town since its prominent members were disappeared at the end of the 1920s. The Georgian homes had long fallen away to sleek white buildings with tinted windows and gleaming neon posters. The wind picked up from the ocean, carrying all the scents of fried seafood from the ridiculous tourist-trap mockery that was the Innsmouth Pier. Kids in jean shorts rolled on with roller blades, little yapping dogs on leashes. He only saw one t-shirt with Cthulhu, and it was a bright red smiling cartoon heresy.

Most people didn't even know what happened here, let alone *why*.

He scoffed and turned away from the bus station, keenly keeping his eyes on the GPS on his phone. The rally point would be outside the Gilman House, one of the only sights from Innsmouth's glorious days gone by. He zipped up his black hoodie and tried not to pay attention to the people walking by. The world churned around him as he hummed old hymns between gritted teeth, songs of Y'ha-nthlei dredged up from the pure efflorescent tongues of those who had never left. He turned through the busy streets, imagining himself on some forgotten ancient track in the isolation of the beautiful dark along the ocean floor.

Not even the Gilman House had been spared from the cosmetic heresy that came with modernization. It had been painted over multiple times, now bright lemon-yellow. Its windows had been shuttered, dark brown two-by-fours blocking all light. Weeds snaked in thronging vines across a rotting porch, wrapping themselves across the pillars as ravenous tendrils. It still stood proud, however, defying the weight of its own decaying bones. No change in management or dopey town mayor could ever erase what happened here.

He saw the congressman on the porch of the Gilman House. *He* had the look, white-green phosphorescent skin that probably glowed in the dark, hair slicked black and flaked with sea-salt grey. His eyes were further set into his skull, but no doubt he could protrude them further out if he needed to. He was tall, commanding in a black suit jacket and pink tie.

"We don't need some liberal governor telling us what to do!"

The congressman had a deceptively high voice, laced with a nasally cadence from a shark-fin nose.

The crowd whistled in agreement. His fellows, his peers who understood the true message of the Old Ones and the great comfort of their truth. The men and boys wore black, sigils and rites etched across their t-shirts in jutting white script. They wore sunglasses against the ash-grey sky, screaming their defiance as they stamped their feet with the congressman.

"They will not replace us!" they chanted.

He felt his spirits lift, running to join them as he hastily removed a folded paper sign from his backpack.

"You're *absolutely* right!" the congressman responded.

He had seen videos on YouTube of the congressman doing interviews and making campaign speeches. He saw the one where he supposedly drove that reporter woman mad, but even in that one the congressman didn't seem to have much in the way of charisma. What videos he could find of the congressman on the House floor were either of him sitting impassively behind some speaking member or introducing legislation advocating for religious and personal freedoms. Freedoms that made even the conservatives in the audience pale and sweat with visible nausea.

"They will *not* replace us." The congressman's eyes came forward in his skull as troglodyte, milky-white irises with grey pupils. "My ancestors *built* this town. They're *still* in this town! After what they did to the Marshes, we don't ask for much! We just want to be left to our own and keep to our ways. The *old ways!*"

The crowd went wild in contagious jubilation. The Marshes were heroes, old guards who kept the gates closed from both the wannabe acolytes and the liberal revisionists. It was rare to see a Marsh in public, the congressman being a notable exception. Graced with a sleeker, greater human form, they were as close to demigods as he and the rest of the crowd could stand to believe in.

"They have no right to punish us for something that happened *decades* ago!" The congressman raised the megaphone to his narrow, dark lips. "The Gilman House is the victim of a conspiracy to pave over what we built. Multiple changes of mismanagement, but no new owner could withstand the libel campaigns against them.. The fake news media has a way of embellishing the past when its suits them but ignoring every good thing families like yours and mine did for this country!"

"The Marshes are *killers!*"

The voice screeched from a rival megaphone. The woman wore blonde dreadlocks with a stitched pink hat. His eyes were drawn to her green t-shirt, a crude elder sign drawn across her chest with the phrase "That which is not dead should get there fast" in bold red print.

She was flanked by legions of the teeming ignorant holding signs they didn't understand and shouting slogans they recited from their televisions and their pulpits. There was a variety among them, ranging from the college senior to the nearly deaf elderly chaplain. The so called "right" and "left" had a way of uniting against the truth, of repressing the worst kept secrets in history simply because those secrets threatened their cultural hegemony.

"I see the media sent their flunkies." The congressman's voice was being drowned out by shouting, curse words and curses flying up from dueling circuses.

"Curious how the police aren't here to protect lawful protestors. No doubt the governor willfully ignored my request for the National Guard!"

He looked around, not sure if he saw any police officers but willing to believe what the congressman was saying. It wouldn't be the first time the federal government withheld protection when the Innsmouth diaspora needed it.

"The violent hordes of the illogical," the congressman pointed, "embracing a future that's already broken, willing to march us to our end for the sake of causes that haven't worked and never will just because they believe in a social justice that–"

Somewhere there was a scream of terror, a high shriek of someone hurt and confused. Then silence hung in the grey summer air. He looked around, for a moment seeing everyone still around him. They looked to each other, afraid and unsure until the next voice spoke up.

"They threw a *fucking brick!*"

The silence was swallowed in an incoherent roar.

Protestors and counter-protestors threw themselves against each other. He picked up a rock, ready to defend himself. Someone rushed him, someone whose face he didn't have time to see before he swiped up and knocked their chin back. He had enough time to glimpse at their shirt, to see the phrase "Dagon is the Devil" and the cross hanging around their neck.

He moved backwards, slamming into bodies as he tried to fight his way out of the crowd. Smoke canisters popped into the sky, and the black uniformed riot police moved in with shield and sticks. He coughed, bringing his sleeve to his mouth as tears welled out of his eyes.

He ran and kept running until he was somewhere quiet and calm.

He was out of breath, looking around to see he was in a part of Innsmouth that the globalists had claimed. Over the gentle strip mall gossip of seaside visitors he heard the wail of sirens. News would spread quickly. The police would want to question everyone involved.

He took out what little money he stole from his mother's purse and walked into a department store.

...

He wasn't sure where he would go from Innsmouth; home, he guessed. He didn't think he'd hurt anyone, not in a serious way, at least. And it had only been self-defense. He had no love for people like that, but he didn't want to be responsible for killing them. Hurting them was tolerable, but the idea of someone's neck snapping from a rock to the chin made him queasy and terrified.

He'd spent some time crying in the Starbucks bathroom, stifling his heaving sobs and rubbing his tears with rough brown-paper napkins.

Yeah, he'd need to go home.

This wasn't for him. This was too much.

He'd have one coffee, one drink to keep him awake for the bus ride. To keep him alert while he made his way out of the city.

He got to the front of the line, ready to hand his wadded dollars to the too-young clerk when he heard the voice behind him.

"I'll get the young man's coffee, if that's okay?"

Congressman Marsh had an even more commanding presence in person.

He felt his stomach flutter, hungry and queasy all at once.

The clerk didn't seem to recognize him, only smiling uncomfortably at his greenish skin and blind-looking eyes. Behind him, two Secret Service agents remained impassive, earpieces receiving communications from some headquarters where seats of power were still preparing for the congressman's inevitable ascent.

"Th-thank you, Congressman."

"Please," the congressman smiled to reveal slightly pointed shimmering white teeth, "call me Robert."

"Right...*Robert?* Thanks for the coffee."

"Son." The congressman clapped his shoulder and motioned to a booth.

"I saw what you did at the rally."

"Oh...is he okay?"

"Between you and me"—the congressman leaned in, hands holding up a wide, drooping chin—"it doesn't much matter. Those people, they weren't *us*. They're the worst this country has to offer, right?"

"...Right."

The congressman nodded. "That's a good boy."

He flagged down the barista, seemingly unphased when she somehow managed to mispronounce "Marsh" as "Mersh."

"Power doesn't always have to announce itself, that's what Maggie Thatcher used to say," the congressman started, bringing a coffee to his lips and staring out as the rain began to roll over Innsmouth and the sun began to set.

"Power could be quiet, real power could. That's how the Marshes held on after the raid. We were quiet, we were patient. But political correctness is getting out of hand. They're going to use it to take *everything* from us. The town may have voted to remove the Gilman House, but it's *not right*. You can't take that much from people... That's why I ran for Congress, why I plan on winning the presidency. I want to leave this world a better place."

"That...means fewer people on it, right?"

The congressman stopped at his question. A wide scimitar-smile exposed his teeth, pulling the flesh that could be gills tight around his neck.

"What are you going to do, son?"

"I'm gonna vote for *you*, Congressman."

The congressman laughed, a loud, throaty chuckle that echoed in bullfrog bellows across the coffee shop.

"I appreciate that, but I could use more than votes. I've got a planning committee here in Innsmouth. We'll be meeting in the Temple of Dagon in about an hour and a half. Think you could make it?"

"I...I need to catch the last bus out-"

"That shouldn't be a problem."

"All...all right."

"Great. Well, son," the congressman stood up and flattened his pink tie, "I'll see you there."

He stayed behind, too nervous to drink his coffee as the rain poured down harder in thick waves.

•••

The Temple of Dagon was new, the original paved over and renovated many times. The order no longer had any aspirations for esotericism, now reveling in the sensationalized image created by reporters who could not penetrate its inner membership. The Innsmouth temple was like many others, obsidian black with crimson red windows and gothic spires jutting upwards like knives into the sky.

He had never been in a temple before, had never felt the need to commune with the wonderful, apathetic beings who he already knew well. He had read a few books, participated in some discussions online. He had thought that had been enough until now.

Entering the temple's double-doors, he felt a power fill him. The presence of beings greater and older than mankind was woven into every disorienting angle of the architecture. Where there would normally be corners there were only round, golf ball-sized holes to prevent the infiltration of Tindalos hounds. There were tapestries, things welling up from the seas and descending from the stars to feed on men and women who smiled with euphoric bliss at their own destruction.

"What are you doing here?"

The young woman was not what he expected. She was sharply dressed, uncomfortably pretty and dagger-eyed.

"I'm here for the congressman's planning meeting," he said, finding his voice weak and fluttering.

Her scowl melted into a smile. His legs went rubbery as she spoke in a sweet, Southern-laced hospitality.

"Well of *course* you are! If you'll just follow me."

He followed her for what seemed like ten minutes, moving through the catacombs of the temple, immersing himself in the impossible architecture of a building of boundless stairs. They descended flights of steps which became less intricate and more primitive as they entered deeper into the earth. The electric lights above them gradually fizzed and vanished, replaced with orange-burning torches that only crudely and half-heartedly eliminated the darkness around them.

His guide finally stopped him before a set of wooden doors, ornamented with iron-knockers in the shape of a blind, fanged fish.

"They'll be waiting for you."

Without waiting, his guide left, not giving him a moment to turn around for one last look at her as the doors opened wide.

The congressman smiled wide, the black robe flowing from him with gold-and-red laced swirls depicting the shapes of galaxies faraway and never seen by human eyes.

He followed the congressman's beckoning, walking down pews of darkly dressed men and women. He had never seen so many people with the look before, and had never imagined that so many were still alive in Innsmouth. They all wore the same grin, an eager sign that they believed their triumph was soon and inevitable.

He sat next to those like him, the congressman's guests who returned the same eager, nervous smiles. They were out of place, wearing black jeans and torn shirts, but were all proud to be willing soldiers in the fight for a glorious truth.

The congressman ascended a pulpit. Behind him was a wide pool of deep, brackish water glimmering back the wavering lights of the torches behind him. He had heard stories about these, the long, underground caverns connecting inland Innsmouth to the deeper waters of the ocean.

A truly sacred place. He knew his pride was meaningless, but he could not stop the faltering smile on his face.

"Brothers and sisters," the congressman began. "We are on the precipice of our final victory. Outside the cattle sing about the polls, about the mathematical impossibility of the victory we are soon to achieve. We will soon lead this world into a bright future, back to an even brighter past."

A chorus of shouts and ribbits erupted from the congregation.

"What we saw today in Innsmouth is the result of centuries of seeds planted, of a long great plan to align the stars. The tensions are ripe, a bloodletting is coming! Iä! Dagon! Iä! Shub-Niggurath!"

He attempted to chant along with them, horrified he had been mispronouncing the names of his deities for so long.

"I'll now invite our honored guests to join us on stage, so that they may aid us in our goal to rewrite this reality."

He breathed quickly, butterflies in his stomach. He was doing *something*, finally escaping the immobility of his computer screen to take part in a movement bigger than himself. He would stop them, those social justice warriors who wanted to repress natural law because they knew it would tread them beneath its righteous heel.

He turned to face the crowd, their sharp smiles and wide, bulbous eyes peering out from their hoods.

"I invite our daughters to rise up. To aid us in our ritual."

From the pulpits they stepped forward, thin shapes in flowing robes. They stood across from the guests, facing them and inviting them to receive their outstretched hands. He took the hand of his partner, repressing the warmth of his blush as he attempted to peer beneath the darkness of her hood.

"Though we may never receive the favor or interest of our gods," the congressman continued, "we now ask for their *strength*. For their *power*. Let our sacrifices be glorious statistics toward our final victory."

His partner shook her hood loose.

His heart sank, blood running cold at the sight of the leader of the counter-protest.

Of her blonde dreadlocks and stitched pink hat.

She grabbed his shoulders and lunged on him, pushing him down deep into the dark, briny waters.

He tried to fight her as her human façade slipped away, but she was iron beneath the waves.

As his lungs filled with water, he had one last look at the face of a smiling, uncaring god.


**Author's Notes:**

This was a story written in response to moment that made me mad, written after Charlottesville. The main character isn't named because he doesn't deserve one. I have no doubt that some people will read themselves into this story. People who complain about diversity in politics and literature. People who twist their hands every time racism, and its relationship to power and literature, is brought up.

This story isn't an attack, not on anyone or anything. But it is a response. A response written after one of the ugliest moments I had seen in my life.

# The Ambassador in Yellow

ELENA CARTER BELIEVES her president is the greatest man who's ever lived.

For too long, the world has been led by the useless, men and women clawing at a darkness eating them alive even as they rage against it. For too long, it has been ruled by the liars, the coddlers. Mankind has grown comfortable, fat, and complacent. Untenable, unsustainable delusions of grandeur have permeated its collective conscience.

Humanity has forgotten that it was nothing at all but cosmic dust.

The president will remind them.

Elena believes in her president's vision. In his truth.

There is no greater universe, no greater revelation beyond the carnivorous black. There is no fighting the chaos, no staving it away with tawdry signs and symbols. Better to supplicate herself at the feet of the only truth that mattered.

So she loves her president, who loves her more than the man on the wooden cross ever would. He represents *everything* to her. A way to escape the meaninglessness by giving in to it, a way out of her family's dying farm and the withering town around it.

Her president was the voice of a god. A god whose single mercy would be granting the world the annihilation it had so selfishly denied itself.

She loves her president, but the journalists do not.

The journalist on the other screen hates her, too. Elena does not blame him. He wants answers to his questions, answers that he and most of the country know. As long as she and everyone else in this administration say just enough, the doubt will remain. And the great untruth will hold. As long as she does not tell him what he knows, men and women across this dying country will throw themselves between the president and anything that would do him harm.

Whether it be a bullet or something so inconvenient as the truth.

How could they explain the death of respected journalist Jenn Mahnken? The dead graduate student at Miskatonic University? The Innsmouth riots? How could the president *possibly* argue that the nihilistic Cthulhu cultists, known for terror attacks across the United States, are "very fine people indeed"?

Elena smirks. Blinks twice.

"It is not the president who controls the stories," she begins. "The president does not finance the media. He is a famously humble man, famously forthright in his religious convictions. For as much as the media fear the president, he is hardly the power that *they themselves* are."

The journalist scowls and raises his voice. She continues.

"The swamp-dwellers want an enemy in the president because it is good for their ratings. For their viewers. They want an enemy in the president because the vitriol is as great as any other opiate. And quite frankly, you smile, you *don't care* that they hate the president. The *president* certainly doesn't care."

The journalist's lip trembles.

He is pathetic.

But what about the president's tweets? What about the strange symbols that, within the first fifteen minutes of being seen, drive those who read them into a violent rage. Four Americans, the journalist reminds you, died because of the president's tweets.

She scoffs.

"Surely you don't blame the actions of a few disturbed *individuals* on the president?"

She tells him that that he is doing him a favor, that despite all his pleading there is no law that she or anyone else in this administration must bring themselves to *his* show. Answer *his* questions.

And he shouts.

And she shouts back.

By the end, the journalist's face is sweaty. Veins throbbing along his forehead. He cuts her off and the interview ends.

•••

General McIntyre despises Elena, just as he hates nearly everyone else in the White House. Elena doesn't care too much for him either. His nose is too pointed, eyes too grey and narrow. In another world he would have been a hunter, a battlefield monster. He was accustomed to speaking in the incantations of ash and fire, not ready for the sliding tongues from just beyond the void. With great swinging steps that make the medals on his chest jingle like so many windchimes he walks up and down the West Wing, complaining about the smell and roaring at any creature unfortunate enough to walk too slow.

It is a good thing, then, that Elena has earned the favor of her president.

The general only spares her a wrathful look as she walks straight past him and into the oval office. She shoots him a smile, one further lash for a broken, defeated animal.

In the golden-yellow light through the curtains, the president's skin seems to shimmer. Since winning the election he has only grown taller. His black suit matches the jet black of his hair. He smiles and her stomach flutters.

"Great job with Cuomo."

His teeth are grey-white, vaguely pointed and serrated like a great white shark's.

"It ought to drive them *crazy*."

It was part of the divine plan, to drive humanity to claw its own eyes out. To deny reality so much that it was remade. To subsume the world first in lies and then in water.

"*Iä Cthulhu*, Mr. President."

"*Iä Yog-Sothoth*," he replies, lukewarm and bored.

He sits down, gesturing to a white couch so that Elena may sit as well. When she does, he wastes little time.

"They beat me in the midterms." He looks to the flag beside him and snarls. "It was little more than a meek death-screech, but one that was heard nonetheless. Our friends in the court did not...assist as they have promised."

His wide eyes fall on her.

"I would like you to meet with the ambassador. Carcosa's consulate leaves me with a few questions. I need to know where we stand."

Elena would already do anything for her president. She loves him more desperately than she ever loved her father, her husband, or her former God. She would give her life for him, and compared to that, looking upon the Yellow Sign seems a small, insignificant sacrifice.

...

The court's consulate is swarmed with protestors, as it is every day. The consulate is a tangled mess of ivory-white spires, smooth and corner-less towers like so many horns and tentacles. Rotten-yellow stained-glass windows break across the daylight, outlining figures in white robes and golden masks.

A few recognize her, hurling every insult that their simple mouths can form. Elena whispers an old word and a few women crash to the ground, holding their heads and screaming out curses. In the crowd, they're swallowing their tongues, hands scraping at their throats until they're red and ragged.

Vermin. Vermin that have every right to the deaths they've thrown themselves into.

The Golden Guard stand tall against the wooden doors. Their black robes have no sleeves, their masks hanging like long, gilded pharaoh's coffins. She walks between them and the whispers snake around her in icy tendrils.

She enters through the wooden doors and immediately succumbs to a rush of vertigo. The hallways are wide, Gothic, and dark. The medieval cathedral roof seems to reach far higher on the inside than the outside. All the grey-yellow windows seem too far away, corpse-colored embers of dying stars.

The whispers continue.

Living shadows snake their way along her ankles.

She mewls, scratching the skin beneath her long hair.

She cannot succumb to the court. The court is merely a distraction for its king, and the king is lesser.

Lesser than her president. Lesser than his gods.

She stands, knees shaking. She looks forward to the darkness, keeping her eyes away from what little light there is.

The emissary arrives before her, a sudden eruption of song and golden light. She wears shapely robes, a gilded veil that jingles with the slow movements of her face. She towers over Elena, craning her back to get a better look.

"H-hello."

The emissaries are famously silent, only emitting songs in a dry, scraping language.

"I'm here to speak with the ambassador, on orders of President Marsh."

For a moment, Elena does not know what the emissary will do. The last ambassador to Carcosa returned to the White House as little more than a skeleton. He collapsed in the Oval Office, a branded Yellow Sign carrying the vague odor of burning flesh. Since that time, her president has not filled the position, though the court still has a direct line to the Oval Office.

The figure swirls and walks forward. When Elena is still it turns its head. A long, white finger beckons her to follow.

The ambassador's office is a semblance of normalcy. Four walls, comprehensible geometry. A wooden desk stained yellow-brown. A couch and two chairs.

The ambassador himself is a jaundiced, tall man, with a long face and narrow black eyes. His brown-white hair is thinning, combed to the right. But it's his suit that unnerves Elena the most, the swirling patterns of golden universes across a sky that's almost *too* black.

The door behind her slams shut, and Elena is left alone with the ambassador.

"Have a seat."

He motions to one of the onyx-black chairs.

She tries to muster her courage. "The president wants to know why he lost the midterms."

The ambassador's face does not change, does not respond to the accusative tone just beneath her voice.

"By the court's estimation," he whispers, "it is because more people voted against his allies than for them."

"You know what I mean."

"Very little," the ambassador responds curtly. "You mean very little, Elena Carter. To the court. To 'your president.'"

"Then why help us? Why hack reality to begin with?"

"The King in Yellow's interests are simple: Disruption. Chaos. Subversion," The ambassador's disinterested, dry whisper continues. "Robert Marsh promised to bring all of this and more. But they were hollow, meaningless promises. Nonetheless, the court decided to reward him for making these promises at all."

"'Meaningless'? How can you say that with everything he's done?"

The ambassador places his hands beneath his chin and leans in.

"The court will admit that Robert Marsh has been a loyal servant. But it is above his station to expect the court to hold his hand. He cannot fathom the will of the king, nor discern the machinations of the swirling nuclear chaos. He is as little to us as you are to him. Why he would expect anything from us is beyond–"

"He allowed the court to build here!" Elena interrupts, her teeth scraping tightly together. "No president before had ever acknowledged Carcosa's sovereignty claims, let alone allowed it to build in this physical plane! He gave you–"

"Nothing was his to give. It seems the boy must be reminded what he is. The court will find these sorts of annoyances to be intolerable in the future."

The cold along her shoulders is searing. The long claws dig into her coat and her skin below, pin-prick bubbles of blood dribbling down. Her stomach seizes as the white fingers dig further in, emerging slick and covered in pink.

More hands come to her face, prying open her eyes.

She screams, but the ambassador is impassive.

He languidly reaches into his desk, removing a piece of paper and a sickly yellow pin.

She cries out, attempts to turn her eyes away.

But the ambassador simply traces his sign into the paper.

When she sees the Yellow Sign, her sight is engulfed in light.

•••

When he hears the recording, General McIntyre pities Elena. He's no stranger to torture, to the sounds men and women make when they are ground and torn apart. But in Elena Carter's screams there is something he does not recognize, an alien panic that he did not expect from someone who already *knew* what she was getting into.

Elena was like too many of them, believers in a cause that the general would never understand. Every day he thought of leaving, of abandoning his president and the country that had made this foolish, irreparable decision.

But he listens to her screams.

And he stays.

He knows his hope is foolish, but it's the only thing that keeps him going.

The recording comes to a merciful end.

He clicks it off and turns to the president.

There is a fury in those grey eyes, an undeserved indignation.

"Mr. President, we need to respond."

"And say *what*, General? That we're going to war with Carcosa? Pure folly."

"Not war, but we can't let this go unpunished–"

"We can. We will."

"Sir!"

"General, I promise you that for all the horror you think you've seen in your life, I can show you *more*! I promise you that I *will*! The court's actions are not even a setback, only a reminder."

"That the President of the United States is beholden to a foreign power!?"

The president laughs into a coughing fit.

"And what are *you* beholden to, General?"

The general does not speak.

"The President of the United States."

The general looks to the floor.

"Don't worry, General. You'll be there for the end. You all will. You're dismissed."

The general takes his leave, closing the door as the president begins his prayers.

In vain, the general makes his own.


**Author's Notes:** Congressman Marsh was supposed to be funny. He was supposed to be a joke, a one-time thing. He was never supposed to be *president*.

The idea to set an embassy from Carcosa came up because, to my horror, I found that I had not written a King in Yellow story. It was supposed to be a humorous, the idea of the King in Yellow being a foreign power manipulating the US presidency. I mean, if it were truly this cosmic power, why would it bother with something like the presidency? The whole notion is ridiculous.

To this day, I don't know how or why the death of Jamal Kashoggi worked its way into this story. But here we are. It was really a moment, for me, where I truly understood how powerless I could feel. Here was a renowned journalist, lured to an embassy and tortured to death. The evidence was there. A recording exists. And yet, there was nothing to be done. Not much that *I* could do, sick and horrified as I was. Sure, I could protest outside an embassy. I could write my congressman and senator, even the White House. But that didn't, and still doesn't, seem like much.

I hope this is the last story in the "Congressman Marsh" cycle. But we live in a scary world.

# The Darkness Makes Us Whole

## I

I IMMEDIATELY REGRETTED the way my conversation with William Dumont ended. He had come into my office with an already dimmed enthusiasm, worn down by gossiping amongst the faculty and snickers from the graduates and undergraduates beneath him. He remained determined out of defiance and a genuine passion for his scholarship, the qualities which we try to instill in our students but we also are trained to ruthlessly cut down.

It was the middle of October, three years ago, when William made his final effort to persuade me on his dissertation topic. The Miskatonic Department of Literature was bearing the fruits of the new hires it had made ten years ago. The realists, new, classical, and magical, came to outnumber the rest of us by the time William was admitted into our program. He and the rest of his cohorts were fed the typical rejection of fantastic or even remotely unrealistic fiction by those scholars of Dickens, Tolstoy, and Hugo who I am forced to call "colleagues." However, I found them more to be like hyenas, tearing at the corpse of the old department heads who hired them.

William, only 21 and already able to debate Shakespeare with Dr. Pontis (who is the only remaining faculty member who I might call my senior), immediately struck me with his knowledge of both authors and their lives. Originally, it seemed his research would gear towards the comprehensive study of author autobiographies. When he came into my office to simply talk about the sad life of Edgar Allan Poe and the disappearance of Ambrose Bierce, I knew that I had found a comrade of similar literary taste. As one of the final surviving academics of horror fiction, I appreciated the sincere interest William gave my research.

But when the time came for William to propose his own research, he had developed a sort of mania.

It was cold that day, white frost clinging to the collar of the long black coat that accentuated the paleness of his hands and face. The sky had been bright outside my horizontal slit of a window, but slowly darkness crept in shades of purple and black as William raised his voice, his face reddening with lack of breath, eyes wide with an excitement which unsettled me to my core. His notes were extensive, well over a thousand typed pages of annotations to primary sources, eyewitness accounts and newspaper clippings.

"Professor Archer," he never gained the courage to call me Michael, "the crux of this study is the phenomena of new American mythologies. Sasquatches, the Tcho-Tcho of Burma... I am trying to meld together the foundations of anthropology, sociology, and journalism through the lens of literature. I have eyewitness accounts, the stories inspired by them. All of it is a study of how literature permeates its way into the zeitgeist to meld the popular mind. The same way that *Paradise Lost* reinforced Christianity and the belief in it, I want to look at these twentieth century legends to see how they have left us. What we can do with them."

My stomach sank as I replied, "William...as you show in your notes, this particular University has had firsthand experience with what you describe. Dryer's account of–"

"The *Miskatonic* and the *Arkham*, yes? The 1928 expedition? Yes, Professor, this would be the centerpiece of my study!"

I hesitated, dreading that my criticism and ultimate denial would deal too crushing a blow to a promising, though misguided, young scholar. I paused before continuing, collecting my words into the most delicate arrangement I could imagine.

"Dyer, Wilmarth... These *academics* did irreparable damage to the University's reputation. Do you know that for the first years following Dyer's self-imposed exile from the University, people actually *believed* him? Sure, they were on the fringes, but ultimately when another expedition to the same Antarctic coordinates found no lost city, no carvings, no monsters... Dyer died insane (his Australia story revealed to be a complete fabrication), Wilmarth admitted his fraud and took a generous severance from the University. And those are only the beginnings of the University's history with hoaxes... I assume you pay at least a little attention to the Herbert West story in your study?"

William nodded. An understanding was coming into his eyes, a shadow that slithered from the back of his mind to the fronts of his eyes. His smile was coming undone, and I knew that I could not avoid hurting him.

"You've picked an ambitious topic, William...but you're at the wrong institution to pursue it. Miskatonic, the literature department in particular, has been trying to distance itself from these hoaxes for over half a century. Not only that, but I am not sure it is suited for a *Literature* dissertation. You talk about bringing in other fields and I think–"

"I thought you would understand," William murmured. His face had turned away from me, from his notes, and down to the floor. William was rapidly becoming a photograph of despondency, and I found myself swallowing back my own tears.

"I understand, believe me. Your enthusiasm for this project, the academic merit of it. I *understand and appreciate it*, I even *admire* it. But it is impossible. Impossible *here*, anyway... I think you might want to shelve this project for after you receive tenure."

I wanted to tell him more, that I knew what it was to have peaks of happiness and nadirs of incredible self-loathing; to be inexplicably motivated towards futile exercises only to hate myself after their completion. I understood, I wanted to tell William, how manic depression often works itself into the minds of eccentric genius. That there were ways he could manage and redirect the problem that I now saw writing itself on his face.

But before I could, he slammed his laptop shut, forced it into his bag, and without looking at me screamed, "You don't understand! No one does! I *will* continue my study, even if it is not here!"

He was out of my office before I could reach him. I called after him but the hallway was empty, save for the echoes of his rapping footsteps and the puzzled, angry faces of the few professors whose research had been disrupted. I began to run after him, but reminded myself that in my own episodes I needed time alone.

So, sick with grief and regret, I graded a few papers and returned home.

It was the last time I would see William Dumont for three years.

## II

I began to worry the first week I did not see William. I imagined he would walk through my office doors, or silently intrude into my seminars and sit in the back row as I lectured. I had hoped that though he perhaps would not fully recover from my words, he would at the very least accept his need to move on. He knew that I would write him a letter of recommendation to another university, should that be what he wanted, that I could provide him a salaried research assistanceship if he needed funding while he reassessed his course of study.

After two weeks, I began searching. First I tried email, and when he did not reply I asked my colleagues if they had heard from him, but they only either feigned concern or displayed indifference. After all, they had their own graduate students.

Then, I finally asked one of my students for his phone number. When a dial tone informed me the number had been disconnected, I finally resolved to find his address.

I found that William's apartment was worse than I had imagined. He lived in a low part of Arkham, a neighborhood which had long ceded its pride to a fate of violence and perpetual poverty. Former colonial houses of tall and narrow architecture had been split apart into apartments and hovels. The bright, vibrant colors that could have been were drowned by the greys and browns of disrepair and neglect. Cars which had not moved in decades were parked on the lawns of houses with chain-link perimeters and residents with old, evil stares. Then there was the smell in the neighborhood...food scraps and human excrement thick with a black smoke.

I had known that William would cut corners to fund his research instead of his well-being, but I never imagined something like this.

In the main office of the divided home which William called his, an old woman with only half her teeth told me what I was most afraid of. He left suddenly, she said through a thick wad of chewing tobacco. She was trying to fill his unit. His mother came by though, with a couple of young men, and they moved his things away.

Did she leave a forwarding address in case he was still getting mail? Or a phone number?

...

The following weekend I was in Providence on the invitation of Mrs. Dumont. Lisa came with me, bringing Jordan, who at 16 was less than thrilled with the idea of spending a weekend at her grandparents'. After dropping Lisa at her parents' house, eye-rolling Jordan in tow, I went to speak with Mrs. Dumont.

Given William's living conditions, I expected a level of poverty in the Dumont home. I was shocked to see a more than generous two-storied house tucked safely into the rolling green lawns of the suburbs. There was no gate, no wide driveway or other obscene signs of an outlandish wealth, but a maintained and disciplined home with wrought-iron fences overpowered by deep but carefully groomed ivy. The home, impeccably pristine and white, looked as if it could house two families or more. The door opened, and a little Jack Russell terrier bolted out to greet me.

"Dr. Archer?" From the opened door, Mrs. Dumont's voice carried her weighted sorrow. She took my hand in her own, weak and with a shaking grip, and invited me in for an afternoon coffee.

Her home was ornamented with decorations and framed pictures. Eclectic memorabilia from all over the world manifested in little monuments and trinkets, carefully dusted and polished. On the walls I saw pictures of old relatives in grained-hazy photographs, and vibrant youths (one of them no doubt William) smiling through funny, baby-toothed grins. There was a certain antiquity to the home; polished wood on the railings and walls, a small kitchen from which Mrs. Dumont brought out the coffee. It was all so much better than William's apartment.

"I know," Mrs. Dumont told me. "I would send him money every month. He told me he didn't need it...but what good is money if you can't spend it on your children?" She smiled distantly and tried to change the subject. "Do you have any children, Dr. Archer?"

"Yes, I have two. A boy and a girl."

"Ah. Me too." The melancholy in her voice was contagious, and I thought of Eric. Perhaps, I thought, this was the way to begin the conversation. I told her about my last meeting with William, about how I was worried because he showed signs of manic depression.

"I know, Dr. Archer."

"You do?"

"Yes."

"Was William on any medication?"

And she gave me the tell-tale sigh, the prolonged "no" that only the relatives of the emotionally ill can give, a sigh I had heard given by my wife, by my daughter too many times. I had vowed to never hear it again after a particularly bad episode, and began taking my medication as if it were a matter of biology rather than choice. Mrs. Dumont told me that William did not adhere to the same code.

"He said that they 'dampened his creativity.' His father said the same thing, before he left us. You have to understand, Dr. Archer," she looked at me imploringly, begging me not to think any less of her or her family, "you *must* understand that whatever William has done is not his fault. This sickness runs through the males of his father's family. It's a sad chain, insanity and suicides for as long as we can trace them back... Some have been successful and normal; William had an uncle who I had hoped could be a role model, but he never did recover from his father's abandoning us... He even changed his last name to mine when he was old enough."

"'William Dumont' was not his name?"

"Not his birth one, no. His father's name was William, also. William Dyer III."

And then the history of William Dumont began to unfold, a young man who hated his father as soon as he could talk. Young William had been happy, vibrant for the space of six years before he began the decline into introverted sadness. In his moods he would read books and journals inherited from his father, and at the formative age of ten discovered the original notes of the 1928 expedition to the Antarctic. Since that point, he had developed a fascination with literature and history, but at some points was given over to a hysterical belief that the notes were of something other than fiction.

"He would have dreams, Professor," Mrs., Ms. Dumont spoke from the rim of her coffee mug. "The most awful things I had ever heard, and he could recount them with such detail. Things that are not in those notes, you understand? He would horrify his sister and I, make us sick to our stomachs with the way he described the anatomy of those *things*. Finally, when he was 14, he was put on a new medication and the dreams stopped. I hadn't heard about them again until about a year ago, when he stopped taking his medication."

Eager to lighten the mood, I told her that her son was one of the brightest pupils that I had ever had. I recalled fond stories of his daunting intelligence, his contagious determination, the way he immediately mastered any material or assignment he could consume. She in exchange told me her own fond memories, and for a moment the air of sadness lifted as levity rose. But ultimately, her questions bubbled back to the surface.

"And you are *sure* that you have no idea where he has gone?"

"I am afraid not."

"Was he seeing anyone, maybe a girl who he could have ran away with?"

"Not that I know of." And I recalled that I had never seen William with anyone, nor heard anything from the graduate students. I thought of my oldest, Eric, and how his fiancée probably rescued him from our disease the same way Lisa rescued me. I wondered what good that sort of love would have done for William, who I had decided that I would probably never see again.

"And you'll let me know if you hear anything from him?" She began to sob.

I reassured her as best I could that everything was okay, that I would do everything in my power to find William. I left her with the promise that I would call often.

### III

When Lisa first became sick I forgot my promise. After our trip to Providence, she developed a thick, haggard cough. When she almost choked next to me one night, we went to the doctor and demanded something other than antibiotics. The chest X-ray came back with the horrifying picture of gray hazy clouds inside a white ribcage. Fighting my tears, I demanded to know how something like this could happen, how she could take such a turn for the worse so suddenly.

"Professor Archer," a grey-bearded man only a little older than my wife and I spoke through thin glasses, "it is highly unusual but not unheard of. There is still much we do not know about cancer, unfortunately, but we know it may sometimes progress faster than normal. She probably has had it for *years*."

"What are our chances with chemo?" I asked. My wife had taken a stoic, proud silence.

"I'm sorry," the greybeard answered in a broken voice.

We were given six months, and my life became a series of late nights, doctors' appointments, and housekeeping chores. For a moment I could escape my sadness by helping Jordan with her homework, or putting together her college applications with her. She was growing so beautiful, so like her mother that it broke and healed my heart at once. I encouraged her to spend as much time with her mother as she could, and she did. But Lisa insisted: "Don't stop your lives for mine."

It was easier said than done.

Eric called the house every night. From Miami he told me that Mikey, the one year-old who I was honored to have named after me, was learning to walk, and that Isabelle was loving her job as a pediatrician. I had always wished Eric would live closer to home, the well-meaning but selfish desire of a parent who never wants to lose their child. But, he constantly reminded me, Isabelle's parents were in Miami and so were their jobs. It couldn't be helped.

"But I should be there soon," he told me in eagerness and dread. "I've talked to my supervisor and they are willing to give me extended leave. I..." He swallowed; I could not imagine how hard this was for him. "I think it's important that Mom see Mikey a few times before...before..."

And he would cry. And after our conversations, after we had said our goodbyes, I would hide myself in my office and cry for him. For me. For Lisa. I would not let Jordan see it; no matter how painful this endeavor, I had told myself that I would need to be strong for both Jordan and her mother.

Two months after the sickness began, the hallucinations started. I was at home all day by that time, locking myself in my office for hours while Lisa slept so that I could keep up the semblance of work. The first hallucination came at noon, when the sun was at its brightest and lapped in gentle, soft waves through our windows.

The scream launched me from my studies and back into reality. It was the scream of a flayed animal, something torn open and salted. It did not register with me until I was almost to our room that these screams belonged to Lisa, and I braced myself for the end.

She was lying face up with her mouth contorted into a jagged angle of a hoarse, grating scream. She was looking at the corner of our room, a place where a little crack in the wall gave way to the attic above us, a little crack only a bit more than a hairline. I gently touched her on the shoulder, but she did not respond and screamed without breathing. I called for her, pleading for her to wake up, and when she finally did, my spirits were even darker than before.

"Michael, they are *here*. They were up there, in the attic. I saw them bubble through with their glowing eyes! They're so horrible...but they already have me!"

"Who...*what* are you talking about, Lisa?"

She could not articulate her answer to me. But the black things with yellow eyes were not done with my wife, for their unseen presence was felt in every dark corner, every unlit hallway. I begged hundreds of doctors in frantic phone calls, pleading for a drug that would help her through her hallucinations. Nothing worked.

I moved my study into our bedroom, setting up a little desk so I could maintain the illusion of work and not leave Lisa by herself. When I absolutely could not be there, I asked Eric and Isabelle to come from the room they were renting in town so that Lisa would not be left alone with her unseen tormenters.

Then, one day, she had an episode when Eric was in the room. Walking with him supporting her into a bright, well-lit room, she fell down. He cursed himself as he told me, about how she looked up into the ceiling and screamed in pain and fright. She howled about something swirling, a great mass of eyes and mouths bleeding out from the ceiling to swallow her whole!

"She said, 'Protect me, Eric, stop them!'" he told me in deadened tones. "But I knew that I couldn't...there was nothing I could do for her."

I stopped asking Eric to take any portion of the burden. As the muscle and blood was stripped away by the illnesses, she resembled less the beautiful woman who rescued me and more a pitiful skeleton. I made the decision that seeing her like this was no longer good for Jordan, who I think was relieved when I began sending her to spend time with her friends outside of the house.

The days became quietly ritualistic for me. Spending all my time with Lisa, I left of the rest of the house to clutter and dust. Jordan, I think, cleaned without my knowledge. All the while, Lisa continued to prematurely rot, meat and muscle slipping off of her day by day. I would stare at my screen, at the unanswered emails and empty, blinking pages, and hope that somehow I could escape into them. But all of it was artificial. Meaningless.

So I watched her. For hours.

Sometimes she would lean up in bed suddenly, seeming healthy and happy until she looked at the corner of the room and began screaming. She would point and jab at the air, pleading with me to *just look* at the little hole! I could see it, she explained, if I would only squint my eyes just right. I never did see it though...and eventually her screaming and hysterics stopped. She began simply looking at the crack and her already pale face would tremble. And I would hold her.

She seemed to know when the end was coming, because she asked me to take her out of the room more routinely. I would pick her up, the sore little relic of my wife, and place her in a wheelchair, or carry her down the stairs while she wordlessly winced at each little step. The sunlight was softer then, horribly soft.

When the end came, I didn't expect it.

I was in the kitchen when I heard her. As I ran up the steps, I realized that the screams were different now, as if a multitude of voices were screaming with her, piping and mewling through her own suffering in a mocking melody of cruelty and sadism. I burst through our door and stepped into an overwhelming odor, a thick and sour smell that rumbled with human filth and bile; the stink of age, a hall of corpses that had not seen the sun for decades. The bed was soiled in dark blood, shining like oil in the sunlight and trailing off into the bathroom.

Lisa was in there. Retching, screaming, and weeping between wheezing gasps which fluted through gurgling and vomit. The substance that littered the floors, covered the toilet, was thicker and darker than anything I had thought a human body could make. It bubbled in some places, still hot and oily from her insides. I covered my nose with my sleeve. I will never forget the noxious stink of that room, a fungus bursting open from a worn and dried eye socket.

On reflex, I flushed her vomit and began to hold her hair back when she cried even louder than before; a suffering woman learning that she had been damned.

"Michael..." she whispered. "...It was looking at me."

## IV

What is in a funeral? People dressed in black, a cloudy sky, a hollow church filled with those who suddenly begin to think about heaven and hell. A wooden box; desperate well-wishes. White flowers. A portrait. The kind wishes of a stranger at a pulpit. Songs and memories.

Songs and memories to be buried down in the dirt with the deceased.

Though I would not know it, Lisa's funeral began my decline into unending personal weakness. Every kind word, every well-wish and stated sympathy drove me further into the ground, staking me down in the dark of my own misery until only the eyes of my children could bring me out. Eric and Isabelle stayed with me for as long as they could, but they had a life in Miami and I was not willing to keep them from it.

And Jordan, my beautiful baby girl, she had her own life to begin too. I wasn't going to hold her from it. It wasn't what her mother would have wanted, so I made sure that we got her to college.

"Are you okay, Dad? Are you sure you will be okay, Dad?"

Yes, yes, I was fine. I would be after all. I was still a tenured professor, a happy grandfather, and a loving father. Life would have a lot more for me, I was sure.

"You can come visit me anytime."

Nonsense, darling. You'll have your own friends down there soon enough and I am *sure* you won't want me embarrassing you. I love you, more than you will ever know, but I can't believe that you would want me to just walk into your life unannounced.

"I'll miss you."

Oh...sweetie. I'll miss you too.

I'll miss you so much.

And so I came to the house, to a home that felt strange and alien in its hostile silence, adorned with pictures that belonged to some other, happier man. Deceased dresses hung in the closets, phantom fragrances from long-dead perfumes hung quietly to an oaken desk with no one to sit at it. There was the garden, orphan orchids which I quietly attended to, though it seemed a blasphemous invasion of someone else's sanctuary. I could not bear to see them go, too, all the wonderful colors; losing them would have been too much for me.

It was with that realization that the creeping force first came to me. The force that told me, as I reached for my medication, that there was no one left to stay strong for. Lisa, Eric...Jordan. They were all gone now. And after all, it was true: I thought better without the medication. And soon I would need to return to my duties as professor.

It was then that I heard the long sigh of Mrs. Dumont, followed by that of Lisa.

I abandoned my medication.

...

My return to Miskatonic was that of a brave, sober face. My students thought I was happy, enthusiastic, and full of a remarkable mirth after such a tragic lost. My lectures, the evaluations explained, were full of a new life and vibrancy, a certain intoxicating theatricality that drew them in so that they could all recite the gentle cadences of Poe and the silver-tented stanzas of Baudelaire. My writing had gone down considerably, but so few of my colleagues were interested in what I had to say, and even less of them expected me to recover from my wife's death. Some of them remarked under hushed breath that they were surprised I had not retired altogether.

If they had gotten close enough to smell my breath, they would understand how I got by.

At all times there was a flask next to my heart; in a coat pocket or tucked away in a desk drawer. I had to keep up appearances, so I force-fed myself regularly even though I wasn't hungry with my alcohol-deadened stomach. The first week was difficult, but I found that my flask was my lifeline, my boat away from the grief of Lisa and my own...condition, a little numbness on my brain which made me smile.

Sure, there were those who had suspected, but they did not interfere out of a mix of respect of privacy and the dread of encountering a problem that was not academic. If students reported me to the department head, if the dean ever knew, I am not sure. I do not remember much from that time at all, other than the horror of my own home.

The nights were the worst. I could no longer sleep in that room, in the bed where Lisa had died. I had thought, before taking up the bottle, that disposing of the mattress would be enough; to remove the stain of her ink-black blood from the house might put my mind at ease. But it did not; nor could whiskey or bourbon make me tired enough to go to sleep there. The house became daunting, empty and huge without children or love; the walls and rooms unfolding into a labyrinthine prison which the night permeated through every corner and crevice.

There was no safety in the television, whose inane babble became a dull murmur the more time I passed in loneliness; nor did I feel at home when the lights were on. The only thing I could bring myself to do, my lifeboat-ritual, was drowning in two fists of whiskey before falling asleep on my couch every night, as if I were an unwelcome guest in my own home.

And even then, the house seemed much louder than I had ever noticed.

I don't remember the exact date, or even the exact time that I first noticed the creaking, but I remember how cold I felt when I first heard the sound. It must have been late, 3 a.m. or some unholy hour, when it woke me from one of my stupors. My first thought was that someone was in the house, walking above me on the second floor with light, uneven steps. When I went upstairs, irrationally hoping that either Lisa or her ghost had returned to me, I found I was still alone.

Still alone.

The creaking became worse as winter approached. What began as footsteps became a pulsating current of cracking bones and snapping branches. Sometimes it would begin small and then become rapid-fire, the sound that fireworks make. The alcohol was not enough to cover their silence nor to ensure nightly rest. I would sit up, red-eyed and sobbing, as I hugged pictures or pillows until dawn.

I thought about moving, but the thought made me sick. It would be more definitive, more troubling than burying Lisa had been. It would be her final, irrevocable death. And after all, the home belonged to Eric and Jordan as much as it did myself. I convinced myself that I had no right to sell it.

So I stayed; drunken, depressed, red-eyed, and insomniac for a whole year. I am not sure what I said to keep Jordan from visiting, or to stop Eric from calling, but I know it came from a place of superhuman hurt, disingenuous words that I thought were to protect them from me as much as they were to protect myself from responsibility. I regressed into a private childhood, ill-equipped and ill-mannered, only superficially happy in public, alone in a creaking house.

It was the death of Ms. Dumont that woke me from my nightmare.

It was an email that informed me, with the subject heading, "Katie Dumont." I immediately recognized William's last name, which resonated somewhere underneath the fathoms of alcohol and darkness.

My heart rippled, hoping that someone had heard from William so that I could help him regain his scholastic footing.

Instead it was his older sister, Katie, who informed me that she had been instructed by her mother to invite me to her funeral. Katie told me that her mother had heard through other friends at Miskatonic about the loss of my wife, and that she was very sorry to hear about it, but did not have the strength in her final months to write me herself. She said that her mother would have been honored if I would attend her "final sending off." The subject matter was so sad, so dreary, and yet Katie wrote it with such ease and levity that I wondered if she was even sad at all. The funeral a week away, I responded that I would be there and made up my mind to arrive sober.

The service was small, attended by just a few surviving distant relatives and friends from across the country who had flown a long way to see her off, and Katie Dumont. I did not notice her beauty immediately, it was tinged with a certain strength-in-sadness which I admired above all else. Her dress, black and long, covered everything but her ankles while she left her long brown hair untied so it went down to middle of her back. She was in her late thirties, I was to learn, and had been marked by her family's tragedy in a far different way than William.

"Ms. Dumont." I approached her after the priest had given his final rights over the open grave. "I wanted to tell you how sorry I am."

Her smile was earnest but weak. She rubbed her eyes lightly with the back of her hand, and I could see the marks of redness which she had attempted to cover up with dark make up. "Professor Archer. Thank you for attending. My mother thought very highly of you, for what it is worth. William did, too."

I asked the question reflexively, knowing that I shouldn't. "Have you heard from him? Did your mother learn anything after we spoke last?"

She shook her head, sigh quivering under strain and insomnia. "No...no. I'm afraid not."

"Oh. I'm sorry."

She did not say anything else, and I was left to sit silently in thought and mourning as the rest of the well-wishers approached her. I thought back to Lisa, to Eric, who I had so callously abandoned, and I wondered what they would say at my own funeral. Would they be there, standing over my tombstone, remembering the man who stayed up with them late at night, the man who drove them to soccer games and concerts? Or would they remember the incoherent, hateful drunk who pushed them away because he was too weak to take care of himself?

I suppose that this was the first gift Katie gave me. Though she was to give me more.

...

Katie Dumont contacted me the day after the funeral. She explained that she was sorry that she could not talk more, that she had been very busy at the time and concerned with so many things that thinking about William was too much. She remembered, however, that her brother spoke very fondly of me and invited me to come to her restaurant so we could talk about him.

"Her restaurant" turned out to be a popular, four-star seafood restaurant. The place was expansive, a well-lit two-story building with wide windows and tables neatly decorated in white cloth. On the walls hung beautiful paintings from across New England, little coastal fishing villages with idyllic white birds flying into the sunlight. You could smell the ocean out of shear artistic gentleness. The waiters, all in suits and ties, knew of my arrival and simply nodded to a table close to the kitchen. Katie, still dressed in black out of formality rather than mourning, her hair now tied back rather than long, smiled at me as I sat down across from her.

"Feel free to order anything off the menu."

"What? Are you sure?"

"Absolutely. I own the place, so who's there to argue with?"

Katie then explained, at my prompting, that she had learned to cook at a very young age. Her mother, who had been pampered her entire life the way New England aristocrats were, had not learned to cook until it was too late, and when their father disappeared it was Katie who helped her mother prepare the meals. Her interest was that of a hobby at first, but grew into a passion in her teenage years, when she won competitions all over the nation. Though she had several cooking degrees, she attributed her success to her master's in business from Miskatonic (who could have guessed?) and the inheritance her father had left her, which she used to purchase the property that would become her first restaurant.

"The first place was an absolute sty, I'm afraid. Even a master's in business does not guarantee immediate success. It was me and two other chefs at first, serving out of this greasy little diner. I was thrilled when we had enough positive buzz to use the money Dad willed me and open this place up."

"You've done very well for yourself."

"Well, wait until you try the food. I hope my recipes will impress you. I am told being a prodigy runs in the family. William had his books, and I have my plates."

The name bubbled back into the conversation and the tone immediately shifted. I told her all of my fond memories of William, and she told me some of her own. She told me about the brave little boy who never slept with a nightlight, the smiling boy who became a man too quickly when he hugged his sister and told her that he would always take care of her. The young man who liked to fish, who stayed for days in the library during summer vacation so he could soak up other worlds before having to dive back into his own. Then came the sad stories.

"I've felt guilty," I admitted. "I had hoped that I could find William. I knew he suffered from depression, and I thought I could help him with it."

She shook her head. "William wouldn't take his medication. There was no one that could have saved him but himself."

"You refer to him in the past tense?"

She stopped. The food came out and she stared into her chowder before continuing. "Yes, I suppose so... He would have been home otherwise. He loved Mom so much, there's no way he would have let her go without saying goodbye."

We ate. And the meal was far better than I expected.

•••

I reached out to my children, Jordan first.

Making peace with her was easier than I expected; children can be so forgiving if you give them the chance. When I told her that I had found someone, I was not sure what her reaction would be. Hesitantly, she supported me.

"Everyone needs to be happy, Dad. You deserve it."

Eric was harder, more reluctant to speak with me. I had betrayed his trust in a deeper, more biting way than when I had withdrawn after his mother's death. Eric could understand sadness, hurt, and the desire to be alone, but he could not fathom what he called a "betrayal to Mom."

"Give him time. He just needs to wrap his mind around it," Jordan told me.

So I began regularly seeing Katie, who was Catherine to her business associates. Though she was beautiful, which I came to realize each time I held her hand or she kissed my cheek, it was her strength and intelligence that drew me to her. Her confidence, her inability to take the lesser end of a deal or be treated anything less than exceptional was a strength that rejuvenated me after my long sojourn into the bottle. Sometimes on our dates she would drink a glass of port or scotch, and I would look on thirsty as the back of my throat itched with desire. She would notice and offer me a drink, but each time I was called upon to refuse. When I finally told her of the full misdeeds that I had committed with the enabling numbness of alcohol, she stopped drinking on our dates. I told her she did not need to, but she would not hear of it.

So I became happier then, livelier and more coherent than I had been in my lectures in some time. My colleagues, before impersonal and distant, were emboldened by my sudden change and stopped by my office often as if to capture a bit of my life for themselves. The students too, took a greater interest in my work and encouraged me, albeit indirectly, to begin writing a paper on the satirical nature of Poe's lesser-known works. Before I knew it, *The Humorous Edgar Allan* had become a book project aided by two undergraduates and a graduate student.

On most weekends I would drive to Providence, eat at Katie's restaurant, and continue down to walk through some of the oldest streets in the region. Somehow when we were together, two people characterized so thoroughly by sadness, we were able to abandon the darkness of our collective pasts and walk towards something brighter. We both felt it, I'm convinced, and I began to truly believe that it was what Lisa would have wanted, for me to be stronger and happier than when she left me.

After our dates we would retire to Katie's large apartment in Providence's most up-and-coming neighborhood; trendy enough for her and yet quiet enough for me. We would make love early and talk until our eyes finally fell. It was a young love between two old souls that made ours special.

Unforgettable.

# V

Answering my door at 9 a.m. on a Wednesday, the last person I expected to see was William Dumont. For a moment I could not recognize him, his hair had become long, curled and disheveled, with thick grey streaks running through the black like milky varicose veins. He had grown a beard, thick and prophetic, through which he gnashed his teeth audibly. He was paler, the palest man I had ever seen then or since, with a somehow longer face which even beneath the haggard redness of exhausted eyes I recognized. I gaped, staring at him and then letting my eyes fall to the strange symbol tied to his neck, a pendant that looked like a tangle of snakes centered on a mass of teeth with a single eye in its mouth.

I could not find the words to even say hello, so he let himself walk past me. The air behind him carried the matted aroma of bile and the sweet scent of rotting fruit. I gagged, but overcame my revulsion with amazement. He sat down on my couch, crossed his legs, and looked at me expectantly to follow.

"I suppose you are wondering where I have been, Dr. Archer."

"Well, William, yes... Yes! For God's sake, William–"

"Professor, don't be absurd." He spoke coldly, glaring from beneath his crown of black hair. "There is no 'God.'"

"William...your mother is *dead*."

"I know, Dr. Archer," he responded, distantly, indifferently. "I was there at her funeral. I saw them put the corpse in the ground. I saw them give her the rights. I am well aware."

"I didn't see you there." I began to overcome my astonishment.

"You wouldn't have, no. But I was there, I promise. But I am not here to talk about my mother or her funeral, I am here to talk about our last conversation."

"Oh?" I was immediately sad, believing that Daniel had carried a grudge with him for years.

"I understand what you were trying to tell me then. People would need convincing that my project was important, that it actually had any scholastic merit to begin with. You believed in my potential, just not the direction I was pointing it in. But you were wrong, Professor."

"I was?"

"Yes. In a way." He paused, moving his hands together so I could see that the same symbol, the same mass of intricate lines and triangles which filled me with a cold curiosity, adorned both of his ring fingers as well. I looked into his eyes, darker and more intense than I remembered.

"My project, Professor, had no scholastic value. Of that I have become convinced, but...my direction was true. 'Where have I been?' I have been out *there*." He smiled now, revealing teeth that were too white and too sharp. "I have been exploring the world. I have found proof, scientific proof, that what Dr. Dyer had written all those years ago was not fiction. It was fact! Though even he got some of the details wrong."

He chuckled for a moment. "Who was *he* to understand them? To try and interpret them? No...no, Doctor. The 'Shoggoths' (in truth they have no names, no need for them) are something altogether different from what he believed. True, they began as slaves, but they quickly surpassed their masters. Immortal, living miracles!" His eyes were darting about the room, seeing things that I couldn't.

I reached into my pocket, ready to call the police if I needed to.

"William..."

"Don't talk to me as if you pity me!" He spat at me with the animal hatred of a wolf that will not share a carcass. "*Me!* Who has seen the temple of Leng, who has been to the darkest shores of Kadath! I, a high priest whose doctrine you cannot even fathom! It is *you* whom *I* pity, and for this reason alone, I have come to speak with you. I have no need of a degree, no need of esteem! But...you were kind to me once, and I am a faithful friend, if anything else."

I did not know what to say. So I nodded slowly, and with dread I let him continue.

"They eat our own darkness. They fill the empty parts of people, stripped away by time and illness, they make us whole." He looked at me and I could swear for a moment that he was sad *for me*. "They told me that you have the same condition that I used to have. They've cured mine, they'll cure yours too. All you need to give them is time."

A creak in the floorboard jolted me away from entertaining his words as reality. Of course he knew my condition, most depressives can recognize it in each other after one conversation, or one bad episode; and William had spent enough time in my office to recognize the same illness in me that he struggled with himself.

"William," I struggled for a method by which to continue, "have you told your sister you are back?"

"Ah. Yes." He smiled, beamed at the mention of his sister. "I understand that you and Katie are dating now. No, no, don't be worried! I'm actually quite happy. She is my sister and deserves someone good, and I can think of no finer man than you. But no, I have not told her yet. I am going to see her today, please do not call her. I want to surprise her, just as I have surprised you."

He was pleased with himself, a child who had pulled off a great trick. He dusted his lap, sweeping invisible refuse from his great black coat before he stood up and nodded to me. I attempted to mouth a goodbye when he reached my door, but he stopped me once again.

"You may think you have refused a gift. But you have not, for it is already given."

William let himself out, leaving only a sour stench behind.

...

Katie called me that evening.

"He told me he had seen you," she said, fear permeating her voice as much as excitement.

"Yes, yes, he dropped by this morning... Katie, what did he tell you, how did he seem?"

"That is the strange thing...he was *happy*." She fluttered in her breathing, on the verge of sobs. "I told him about Mom, about everything that has happened to you and me, and he *smiled* the entire time. I asked him why he was so happy and he said, 'Oh, Katie. If only you could know, if only I could show you, you would be happy forever.'"

"Wow...did he mention anything else?"

"Only that he had been traveling, that he found himself. I am just..." I heard the tears breaking from miles away. "I am just so glad he's finally found something to make him *happy*."

I could not tell if she was too happy to have her brother back to notice the inherent wrongness in his presence, or if he had dressed differently when he met her. She did not mention his appearance, his odor, the strange things he had told me about, and said nothing about the strange black clothing he wore. Had he intentionally changed his appearance for me? I decided it was best not to remark on it for now, to let her simply be happy that he was home safe.

"He's home, Mike. He's finally home."

...

After William returned, it was Katie's turn to become sick.

It was a horribly familiar scenario: Her coughing next to me one night so fiercely that she could not breathe; a hazy mass in a demanded X-ray, an accelerated death sentence given by a doctor who was uncomfortable even saying the *word* "cancer."

A heavy heart. A resolve to be strong for my children. And for William.

I waited with Katie in the hospital most days, bringing up a lunch from the cafeteria so I could sit with her and talk. She told me things that she wouldn't tell anyone else, that she was afraid to die and that she was too young and that secretly she sometimes convinced herself that she hated her mother for giving her a disease that she knew was not entirely genetic.

I, of course, had no words of comfort and could not comfort myself. Her end would be painful, I knew it and so did she. I could not tell her that it would be okay, that she would see her mother on the other side, because I had long ago lost my own faith. Every day she lost a little more hair, a little more color in her cheeks, and all she wanted was to see her brother, who did not visit her once.

Then, one day, I received a call from the restaurant.

"Dr. Archer." The assistant manager spoke in a hushed, frantic voice. "Is Katie well enough to talk to me?"

I sighed. "No...no, Brian. How are you?" I asked to dodge the disparity of my own situation.

"Katie, she...gave the restaurant away!" The frustration and panic in his voice jolted me out of my self-pity.

"What?"

"There is a man here. He says he's her brother! But he's the freakiest guy I've ever seen! He's got all the paperwork, a lawyer, the police! She *gave it away!* How the fuck am I going to feed my family? What the hell was she thinking?"

"I'll be right down! Don't let William leave, let me talk to him!"

I grabbed my coat when Katie began to stir.

Her gaze was so distant, so weak, before her eyes fell on a corner of the hospital room. Her eyes widened, mouth falling open so it could tumble out a loud, shrill scream. I abandoned all thought but her, turning to her, stroking her hair and hugging her tightly. But her body was frozen, rigid with terror.

"Eyes! Eyes!"

She convulsed in my embrace, thrashing while I screamed for the doctors to help. Then, suddenly, before they could arrive, she choked, coughing up a thick black mucus onto my back.

She was the second woman I had loved in two years.

And the second woman to die in my arms.

## VI

It was not until two weeks after the funeral that I mustered up the willpower to go to the restaurant. William had a lot to answer for. Enigmatic, perhaps insane, he was nevertheless answerable for the wrong he had done his sister by exploiting her to gain control of her business, to close her only legacy. And he had the gall to not visit her on her deathbed, to insert himself into our lives and then immediately leave.

The outside of the building broke my heart, the once wide and beautiful windows boarded up or covered with aluminum foil. The door, covered in dust, did not budge under my touch. However, I had grabbed the key from Katie's apartment and found that whatever precautions William had taken, he had not changed the locks.

The interior of the restaurant was rank with the same horrible scent that William had tracked into my home. It was a raw contagion, an exposed infection that still burst out into the air with an acrid aggressiveness. I covered my mouth with my sleeve and looked around the empty edifice, tables stained with grime, paintings and beautiful carpets torn up in patches and stained with dark blotches.

"William?"

My question went unanswered.

"William? It's me, Michael. We need to talk."

A muffled noise came from the back of the restaurant. It was a mumbling noise, and I thought that William might be calling to me from the kitchen. Pushing through the door and switching on the light, I found that the whole kitchen was covered with plastic and that the floor was slippery with thick black blotches which had clotted and dried. Only then did my mind begin to put the pieces together.

"William?"

The noise came from behind the freezer door.

I pulled the door open and flicked on the light. My mind instantly fled me.

The thing was massive, so tall it almost touched the ceiling. In the vague darkness, I thought it at first to be a man covered in a stained sheet, lumbering in the freezer and squawking madly. But the calls were too deep, too resinous for human lungs. Against my conscious will I began to see the sharpness of a beak, the leathery folds of wrinkled, heavy skin sagging from a lack of fat or blubber. The creature reared its head upwards towards the light, squawking repeatedly as it tried to understand the small source of heat that plagued it. Its body was covered in the same black ichor which only now was familiar to me.

The penguin, the monster of Dyer's account of the Antarctic, lumbered towards the door, towards me, in wide, blind steps. Its massive flightless wings unfolded like arms, knocking over shelves of scalpels and buckets. The noises it made, screaming in suffering and panic between reflexive squawks, were more horrific than any of Dyer's descriptions. Before it could reach me, it doubled over as if in intense pain.

Floundering onto the floor, it expelled the same black substance which leaked out of its eyes slowly. In the puddle, bubbles began to rise.

It was when they blinked that I realized what I was looking at.

I do not know how long I stood there. Too scared to scream, too confused to move as the black substance slunk away from the dying bird. I cannot remember what happened, only that I heard William's voice from somewhere behind me.

"They kill what they can't help. They kill the already healthy, those who they cannot make better. It was a mistake, Professor, to try and help my sister. To try and help my mother and your wife. But you'll understand once they make our world better.

"They've been with us forever, living in the pipes and tubes of our civilization. But now they've decided to help us, to end our self-inflicted suffering by remaking us in their own image. You may think them cruel, but they are organisms just as anything else, and what they cannot fix they must eat.

"You'll understand. You'll feel better."

···

It's only out of courtesy that I'm writing this. Only to give you all fair warning. The healers, they are quickly going to move from the sewers of our world to repair the damage we have made. You may hear them, creaking in your houses or whistling in your pipes, and you may try to rationalize them away. But they are there.

Do not fight them. They make you feel so good, so alive. More complete than you would have ever imagined. Do not worry about your loved ones who may not survive. So be it, they are not worth this type of paradise. Not everyone need make it to the new heaven.

I do not care how this account is published; whether in a news journal or a fiction one is irrelevant. Only the old vestiges of loyalty compel me to write these words, to give an account of what happened so that in the coming months you will understand the process that begins when they invade your skin and scrape under to the rotting foundations of your crippled understanding to make you better than human.

We are, above all else, loyal friends.


**Author's Notes:** This was the first story written in this section, my first published mythos story. Lovecraft has always been a central writer and influence on me, though as evidenced by the earlier stories in this collection I am well aware of his racism and that in his work, which surrounds him. Despite his irredeemable and deplorable views, Lovecraft remains an author who so effectively invokes tone and dread. It's been strange for me to watch Lovecraft slide from the fringe and into mainstream literature. But it's also been quite exciting.

Academia can be mean. Certainly, it is exciting, a hotbed of creativity and creatives. But there is also vindictiveness, jealously, scandals, and rivalries. Dr. Archer is a good professor, influenced by the good professors and mentors I've been fortunate enough to have. William Dumont is the prideful young scholar, someone who insists on reinventing the wheel even though there is no need to.

This is an older story, as I said, and one written in an older style, more directly influenced by Lovecraft than the other stories. Knowing I had an opportunity to write a mythos story, I knew I had to use the giant albino penguins, which are unquestionably my favorite mythos creatures.

# Part III: Brief Goodbyes

2020.

WHEN I WAS putting together my first collection, *Whiskey and Other Unusual Ghosts*, I found that there were stories that just did not fit the mood of what I was going for. For all of my "horror" stories, there were "weird fantasy" stories that just didn't fit. I liked these stories, but they stood out. Certainly, it seemed inappropriate to bring in Clark Ashton Smith, dragons, and Cthulhu into a book that was otherwise made of wholly original concepts. No room for Dracula, vampires, zombies and shark monsters.

So, almost immediately after *Whiskey* was released, I had put together *The Death of An Author*.

This book, like all of us, has its story. It was originally signed to one publisher who championed it. But for reasons beyond our control, the deal did not work out. At the time, I was prepared to shelve the book entirely, at least for a while. I was in Mexico City for research, soon to head to Bogotá. There just wasn't a lot of time to dedicate to finding these stories a home, particularly when I considered it to be an extremely niche book.

I say "niche" because (1) the weird fantasy subgenre is always a difficult sale, at least it seems to me and (2) because many of the stories are "political."

If you are a reader who read any of the preceding stories with something resembling a sense of outrage, I do want to thank you for giving me a chance. But it is a strange thing, being accused of being a "political writer." There is a common, repeated refrain when one is not happy with the political leanings of their favorite writers and artists. "Stick to X, not politics."

To me, this seems a very unfair request. Creative people are, in fact, people. And their thoughts, perceptions, ideas cannot be separated from their experiences no more than anyone else's could. I exist beneath and within political institutions just as much as anyone else, and I also react to politics just as much as anyone else. Fiction, my mode of processing a great many things emotionally, is as much a vehicle for me to process my feelings on the events of the day just as it is my terror of the dark, of sharks, and any other scary thing.

"Sticking to X" is not, to me a reasonable or worthwhile request. After all, if Lovecraft could write about his support of "socialistic fascism" (see "The Shadow out of Time") then why should I not be allowed to write about the terrors of populism, political violence, and democratic erosion?

But, for these reasons, I considered the book niche and was content to let it gather a bit of dust before trying to find it a home again.

Then Scarlett R. Algee reached out, who gets the first "thank you" in this afterword.

Scarlett not only saved this book, but potentially all my work from myself. 2020 was a bad year for all of us, and I did pretty okay, all things considered. I stayed healthy physically, but I went to a dark place creatively and mentally. More than once, I considered just giving up entirely. Scarlett didn't let that happen.

So thank you.

Who else to thank? There are the established folks who encouraged me: Matthew M. Bartlett, S.P. Miskowski, my friendolyn Gwendolyn Kiste, John Langan, Brian Evenson, and so many others. There's the new friends I made in this haze; Laura Mauro, whose story about a space dog makes me cry. There's old friends: KA Opperman, Ashley Dioses, Alan Sessler, John Paul Fitch, Jonathan Raab, John Linwood Grant, Jon Padgett (awful lot of "Johns"), Sarah Walker, Can Wiggins, Russell Smeaton, Mer Whinery, Justin Burnett. The list goes on.

Then there's mom, of course, whose scary books defined my childhood.

And then there's dad, who drove me around North Texas hunting for comics on his free time, even though he still doesn't know Marvel from DC. Who watched ghost stories with me even though he doesn't like horror. Who consistently made every effort to connect with a weird kid who was very different from him, and who still connects with the strange adult that kid became.

I love you, pa.

I hope these stories are less scary.

And now, if you've made it this far, I've got one more story for you.

2020. What an awful, scary year.

# The Last Mayflies out of Bogotá

THE MAYFLIES OVERWHELM the world and make it dark.

We still don't know if it's a new species, generated through some previously undiscovered, accidental mutation, or an infected old one. I haven't paid too much attention to the debates, from scientists or from politicians, who have made several ominous claims about the mayflies. I've been too busy to wonder, crisscrossing Bogotá in green and red TransMilenio buses, packed so tightly that I have to crouch for fifteen minutes, wedged between a crowd of old women who whisper "*pobrecito.*"

I only know that the tourism police have shown up in Candelaria, that people wear masks, scarves, and gloves on public transportation, and that the mayor plans to lock down the city, sending out the police to make sure that people stay in their homes.

In the sudden, mandatory free time when my contacts go silent, I learn about the sickness the mayflies carry. I learn that there is a question as to what exactly the clouds of will-o'-wisp darkness are. Scientists know so little, and can't even tell us definitively if the mayflies are carriers of the disease, or are the disease themselves.

I find it horrifying. Coughing and choking in the dark. Fevers and hallucinations, twisting and thrashing your way out of this dimming world to a dimmer one still.

I don't panic when I see my first mayfly. At first I think it's my eyes, leaving a day of archival research and stepping into the purpling evening sky. It's just a black spot, the size of a grapefruit. When I see it for what it is, I cross to the other side of the street and pay for an Uber.

I buy a mask and gloves the next day.

As the world closes, it becomes uncertain where my "home" is, or where it will be. California locks down its borders, its universities. I'm notified via email that I'll be teaching online. I read that Los Angeles expects to go dark, as dark or even darker than Italy or New York. I call my first home, only for my parents to tell me North Texas is being hollowed out.

This is the first time that the mayflies defeat me. When I realize I may have to go back to my parents' home, a grown man who has been so independent for so long. I don't cry. Not then. I send emails, and wait for my time here to end.

Outside my apartment, the nights in Bogotá are only darker. Soon I can't even see the lights from the neighborhoods lining the Andes Mountains.

The archives announce they are closed on a Thursday.

The president of Colombia announces international travel will be banned. Tourists are ejected from the country, banished for seven years. I begin carrying a copy of my passport and my visa, ready to show officers that I've been in country long before the outbreak reached even the United States.

When I sit in now-eerily empty cafes in Candelaria, I think about the young tourist traveling by herself who I helped order coffee and a taxi. I wonder for a moment if she's okay. Then I wonder, not for the first time, if I am.

I take TransMilenio for the first time since I saw my first mayfly. It's only after the bus begins moving that I see the mayfly. We all crowd ourselves in the back, sweating coldly at the clouds of darkness resting in the connection between cars.

I take a walk at night. There are no bars, no restaurants for me to visit and escape the claustrophobia of my apartment or the leering glow of my laptop. I cannot make out the high Gothic church in Parque Lourdes at night. The persistent, annoying man who offers me everything under the sun is gone.

I realize this is the second defeat. The mayflies have locked me in and cut my research short.

The following morning, the president tweets.

Confused, I call my airline.

This will be my third defeat.

I scramble, throwing everything into my suitcases, gritting my teeth and swearing loudly. I empty my apartment, sending my groceries and whiskey to a friend on the other side of Bogotá. The world is closing, and closing *fast*. My flight is at midnight. In the lobby of my complex, a cloister of dark mayflies gather and rest. I have my mask. My latex gloves.

My Uber driver is a young mother. She is worried, scared and confused. So am I. We amuse ourselves with hurried jokes and small talk. I tell her that I am leaving quickly, that this is my last chance to get back to the United States.

But there are more cases there, she adds, almost a question.

Yes, I say. And I have asthma.

I think about it again. Choking in the dark. Drowning on dry land.

The world is closing and I am running from something. Fleeing. Used to making long-term plans and contingencies to stabilize my anxiety, I merely thrum my fingers against the door handle of the Uber. It's harder to see my last purpling Bogotá sky.

It's when I'm at the airport that I get a call. Verbal confirmation. My new flight will be there. Physically.

Unable to check in, to get through security until three hours prior to my flight, I gravitate naturally towards a cloister of travelers and tourists. I think I have a greying wave on the sides of my brown hair. Certainly, I have it in my beard, small blots of salt against bright copper. But there is an urgency for peace that drives young people together, and before I can sit down with my greasy hamburger I'm waved over and asked where I'm from.

Texas.

The Argentine snickers.

Aren't you all cowboys? she asks. Don't you all have guns?

Well, not *with me*, I answer.

The German laughs at this.

Where did you come from?

Ten hours outside the city. A long bus ride and a whirlwind of phone calls.

Are you okay? someone asks the Italian.

He takes a drink of his soda and just gently smiles.

Satellites don't see Italy anymore. For the first time since Mussolini, there are rumors of mass graves.

The Italian is kind, but he won't stop smiling.

I leave my group at three hours before my flight.

I begin to notice the black clouds in the corners of the room. They grow and shift as a couple screams at an airline official. The Colombian police approach with bright green vests. The couple is removed from the line, weeping and red-faced.

The police meet my eyes and I meekly smile back.

Where are you going?

Dallas.

Why were you in Colombia?

Studying.

Are you sick?

No.

Have you paid the tax to leave the country?

No.

Will you?

I suppose I don't have a choice.

It's easier leaving the country than it was coming in, but more expensive too. On my phone I see that the State Department has ordered all Americans to repatriate or prepare to stay hunkered down and huddled in the dark. An advisor emails me, asking me if I have enough money to live in Bogotá through May, and if I can get my visa renewed if I need to.

I email him and tell him I found a flight home.

I call my family.

It's 6pm in Dallas. Getting darker earlier.

The world is quieter after security.

Around the peripheries of my sight, the mayflies start to buzz.

We're like refugees. The Argentine has found me again; her voice is soft and far away.

I consider what she has to say before she continues, we're running from something.

We *are* running from something.

I don't know, I add. There's a camper that my parents have. I can live there for fourteen days. I'll have hot meals. Hot water. I can work from that camper.

But don't you feel like you've *lost* something, she asks in frank, brusque Spanish.

Yes. Yes, I do.

Suddenly, a closed coffee shop plays fast jazz on their radio. An employee mops the floors, humming to the trumpets and drums behind a grate.

The Argentine invites me over, not enticing but calmly sad. The same as me.

Keeping our distance, we dance. She is graceful. I am clumsy. But we laugh. And as the mayflies swirl around us, so do other desperate eyes.

The jazz ends. I hear some of the taunts from the men and I laugh. A woman's voice says, "*guapo*," and even at twenty-eight years I still blush and smile.

I have a rhythm condition, I explain to the Argentine.

Well, she says, if you're ever in Buenos Aires, I teach a salsa class. It's a good way to meet a girl.

She teases me. But it's friendly.

Our elbows touch and we say goodbye after exchanging numbers. We'll WhatsApp each other when we get home.

I'm so thirsty. My throat is dry, and all the water bottles are gone. The fountains taped off, clusters of black mayflies piled on them.

Are you on a plane? my dad texts.

Soon, I text back.

I love you, he texts.

I love you too, Dad.

We're all running, I think. But only to our houses. To hole up and wait for this to pass. But will it? Or will the mayflies find their way into garages, wiggle their way in the small spaces between windows, infiltrate and contaminate the way bugs always manage to do. Maybe it passes, but how many does it take with it?

Despite my dance with the Argentine, this is my last defeat.

I'm no refugee. But I *am* running. And I *am* scared.

Not only of choking, of dying in the dark, but of the long uncertainty that looms above the swarms of darkening Mayflies.

When I board my plane, when I am seated in a crowded flight with crying children and coughing strangers, I can't see outside my window.

I wonder if I'll be able to see Dallas when I land.


**Author's Notes:** I left Colombia the day the State Department recommended all Americans repatriate or "be prepared to hunker down." It was eerie watching the tourism police shut down Plaza Bolívar, which had been so crowded for all the months I had lived in the city. It was stranger still standing in line for groceries, especially when I knew I would only able to buy groceries for the weekend and no more. Bogotá is usually chaotic, a place of enormous energy. In the last few days I was there, it started to seem like a haunted house.

I wrote this story in response to my emergency departure, my scramble to get back to the United States before the world closed entirely. As I write these notes, we are all still enduring the COVID-19 pandemic. In the United States, vaccines are still rolling out. But in Colombia the pandemic is still raging, and now political and social unrest is exacerbating what is already a delicate moment.

I hope that when you are reading these notes, we (the world) are in a better place. Until then, we flourish. We dance at home, we sing to each other on our computer screens and make grand plans for when we can hold each other again.

Be good. Be kind.

# About the Author

S. L. EDWARDS is a Texan currently residing in California. He enjoys dark fiction, dark poetry and darker beer.